'It's refreshing to enter a world of cats. And ⟨...⟩ but the rich collection of heroes and villains in the world of Varjak Paw . . . *The Outlaw Varjak Paw* is another swift, compelling tale. And Varjak is an appealing and believable hero' *New York Times*

'Varjak Paw is the perfect emblem of the joys and dangers of freedom. Beautifully illustrated by Dave McKean and written in spine-tingling prose, the novels have a suspenseful edginess that children instantly respond to' *The Times*

'Dave McKean's edgy illustrations provide the perfect foil for this elegant and imaginative read' *Publishing News*

'A wonderfully original creation: a fearless feline with a gift for whizzy martial arts . . . Grippingly vivid' *Evening Standard*

'Dark and wonderful . . . Like *Harry Potter* or His Dark Materials, this is a book with true crossover appeal' *Zero Magazine*

'Cats, martial arts, Gothic urban landscapes, bravery, power struggles, creepy towers, juicy fish and some very loyal dogs . . . this book has it all' *Delirium's Library*

'Great new characters and some cracking fight scenes . . . All loose ends are tied up by the end. But you will want to know what happens next!' *CBBC Newsround*

'It's a rare sequel that so surpasses its predecessor; one hopes the neatly resolved plotlines don't preclude further installments' *Kirkus*

www.kidsatrandomhouse.co.uk

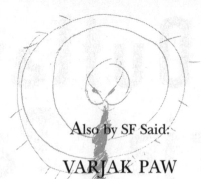

Also by SF Said:

VARJAK PAW

Winner of the Smarties Prize Gold Award

www.varjakpaw.com

The Outlaw Varjak Paw

SF Said

Illustrated by Dave McKean

CORGI BOOKS

THE OUTLAW VARJAK PAW
A CORGI BOOK 978 0 552 55156 4

First published in Great Britain by David Fickling Books,
a division of Random House Children's Books

David Fickling Books edition published 2005
Corgi edition published 2006

5 7 9 10 8 6 4

Set in New Baskerville

Corgi Books are published by Random House Children's Books,
61–63 Uxbridge Road, London W5 5SA,
a division of The Random House Group Ltd,

Addresses for companies within the Random House Group Limited can be found at:
www.randomhouse.co.uk/offices.htm

THE RANDOM HOUSE GROUP Limited Reg. No. 954009
www.kidsatrandomhouse.co.uk

The Random House Group Limited supports The Forest Stewardship Council (FSC),
the leading international forest certification organisation. All our titles that are printed
on Greenpeace approved FSC certified paper carry the FSC logo.
Our paper procurement policy can by found at www.rbooks.co.uk/environment

Extract from *Fragments of Sappho* by Anne Carson reprinted
with kind permission of Random House Inc.

A CIP catalogue record for this book is available from the British Library.

Printed and bound in Great Britain by
Mackays of Chatham plc, Chatham, Kent.

Some men say an army of horse and some men say an army on foot
and some men say an army of ships is the most beautiful thing
on the black earth. But I say it is

  what you love.

Sappho, Fragment 16
Translated by Anne Carson

Chapter One

It was winter in the city. The sun was sinking fast. Night was drawing in. Snow whipped down from the sky in icy flakes. It was too cold for snow to melt, so it covered everything in white: the rooftops and drainpipes, the back streets and alleys.

A silver-blue cat with amber eyes raced forwards through the streets. His name was Varjak Paw, and he was running as fast as he could. He loved being out in the city. He'd grown up indoors, a pet in a house. He'd always dreamed about living free and wild. Now his dreams were coming true.

Beside him ran his friends: a spiky black-and-white cat called Holly, a shaggy chocolate-brown one named Tam, and a huge black dog called Cludge. They knew the city better than Varjak; he was still learning how to survive on the streets. And winter was harsh. Food was scarce. They'd been hunting all day with no luck. Now they were going to the city dump, hoping to find some scraps the people had thrown away.

They swerved into an alleyway. A rusting iron gate loomed up before them, rattling in the wind. It was the entrance to the dump. Far away on some main road, traffic rumbled and roared, but here the cars were all broken down. Their windscreens were smashed, their tyres slashed. Fragments of shattered glass stuck out of the snow. They could rip a cat's paws to pieces.

So this is it, thought Varjak. The city dump.

'Can't we keep hunting?' he said. 'I've got a good feeling. We're going to catch a mouse – we've got to!'

'I wish we would,' panted Tam. 'I'm starving.'

'Me too,' said Holly. 'But we haven't even seen a mouse since this snow started. They must be hiding from the weather. Or from *her*.' She shivered.

Above their heads, through swirling snow, an amber street light flickered into life. Day was almost done; nightfall was close. Holly and Tam shifted about on their paws. Even Cludge seemed nervous.

'Let's get it over with,' said Holly, her voice like the crunch of gravel. 'We don't want to be here after dark.'

Tam looked up at the rusty gate and shuddered. 'Er – why don't you and Varjak go first? I'll stay here and keep a look-out – even if I have to eat last,' she said, sounding very noble.

Holly rolled her mustard-coloured eyes. 'I might've

known. Fine. Come on, Varjak. At least now we know who's scared and who's not.'

'I'm not scared!' protested Tam. 'It's just that we need a look-out. What if *she* comes? It's actually braver to go last. It's actually . . .' She paused, and scratched her head. 'Actually, I think I'll come with you.'

'Oh no you don't,' laughed Holly. 'You're right. We need a look-out – and congratulations, Tam, you've got the job!'

Tam's big, round eyes went huge with fright. 'But – but—'

'It's all right,' said Varjak. He could see Holly was joking; but he could also see that Tam was not. 'I'll be look-out. I'll stand guard, with Cludge.'

Tam's fur settled. 'Thanks, Varjak! I'll save you some food – if we find any.'

Holly and Tam crept forwards through the snow, past hulking smashed-up cars, picking their way over shattered glass towards the gate. Chains and pad-locks hung from it, clattering in the wind. But they found gaps, cracks, ways through that people would never think of. In moments, Varjak and Cludge stood alone.

thud

thud

thud

9

Varjak's fur prickled. He thought he could hear something behind him. A cat's tail thumping? Something was moving, someone was watching him.

He turned. Stared into the darkness at the top of the alley. No one there. Just snow. Rubbish. Plastic bags, scraps of paper, swirling in the wind.

thud

Oh. Of course. Now he knew what that noise was. His own heart, thumping in his chest.

He breathed out, feeling foolish. Tam had made him jumpy. He turned to Cludge.

The big dog wagged his tail. 'Varjak!' he barked. 'Varjak scared of rubbish!' He stretched out a huge paw and swatted away a scrap of paper. 'Not be scared,' he panted. 'Cludge here.'

Varjak smiled. Cludge always made him feel better. After all, what was there to be afraid of when they had a massive dog on their side? Even Holly and Tam were a bit nervous around Cludge, still getting used to the idea of being friends with a dog. Only Varjak had seen the truth: that for all his strength and size, Cludge sometimes felt as scared and lonely as any cat.

'How about you, Cludge?' he asked. 'You OK?'

'Cludge cold,' said the dog. 'Cludge hungry. But Cludge happy with Varjak!'

His tail wagged again, and Varjak felt glad he'd stayed out here, after all. He didn't want to go into the dump anyway. What was the best they could find? Some mouldy old rubbish. That was no way for a cat to live.

He could do better than that – especially if he used his powers. For Varjak knew a secret that gave a cat great power. It was called the Way. There were Seven Skills in the Way. He'd learned them in his dreams, where he'd visited the ancient land of Mesopotamia and been trained by the warrior cat Jalal.

He settled down by a car and closed his eyes. He remembered Jalal's voice, coming at him through the Mesopotamian night. *The First Skill is Open Mind.* Varjak cleared his mind of thoughts. He made himself calm and still, open to everything.

Now the Second Skill: Awareness. He let his senses flow out into the city. He could smell the rubbish rotting, and felt sure there'd be nothing in the dump anyone would want to eat. But his sensitive whiskers also felt a tiny shift in the air currents. Something was moving. Not rubbish; something warm, and near –

A mouse! It was a juicy mouse, hidden just behind that car. His mouth watered; his belly growled. This was what he'd been searching for all day. He imagined crunching into the mouse, sinking his teeth in, savouring every bite –

No. Don't get carried away. Focus.

Hunting was the Third Skill. *When you stalk your prey, you become your prey. You make it a part of yourself.*

Now he was ready. He tensed his body tight, tight. His muscles coiled –

– and Varjak Paw sprang forwards, a silver-blue blur, diving under the car, towards his prey –

– and *WHAM!* There it was, beneath his paws. Fresh mouse, the finest food in all the world.

Holly slouched back through the gate. 'There's nothing good in there,' she sighed. 'It's disgusting. But hey . . . what's that you've got?'

'What does it look like?' he grinned.

'Oh – Varjak! You found one!' Her mustard-coloured eyes lit up. She licked her lips – and then stopped. 'But how are we going to share it out, between us all?'

Thud.

'What you're going to do,' said a brash, loud voice behind them, 'is give that mouse to *us*.'

Chapter Two

Varjak turned. Oh no.

There were four cats at the top of the alley. Big brawny cats with short bristling fur. They swaggered forwards through the snow, tails thudding behind them.

'It's a patrol from Sally Bones's gang!' hissed Holly.

Sirens wailed in the city night. But Varjak and Holly couldn't run. Tam was still in the dump.

'Tam – come on!' urged Holly.

Cludge whined softly, crouching down in the rubbish as the patrol crunched through the snow towards them. Varjak could taste his friend's fear on the sharp, cold air. Or was it his own fear, quickening his pulse, stiffening his spine?

Sally Bones wasn't among them, but Varjak recognized two of her captains. Leading the patrol was Luger, a grey cat with a flat snub nose and emotionless eyes. He looked perfectly calm and poised, but

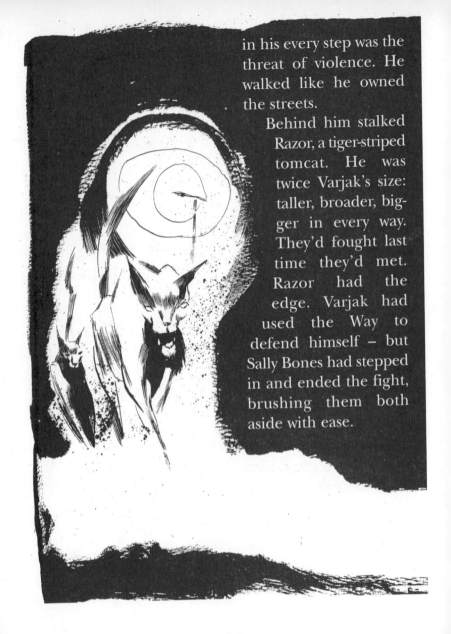

in his every step was the threat of violence. He walked like he owned the streets.

Behind him stalked Razor, a tiger-striped tomcat. He was twice Varjak's size: taller, broader, bigger in every way. They'd fought last time they'd met. Razor had the edge. Varjak had used the Way to defend himself – but Sally Bones had stepped in and ended the fight, brushing them both aside with ease.

Varjak still remembered the thin white cat's ice-blue eye, burning into his mind; still heard her voice, echoing in his head: *Where did you learn that? Who taught you?* Because that was when he realized the Way wasn't just his secret. She knew it too.

'Varjak Paw,' said Luger, his voice cold as metal. 'And Holly. What are you two doing here? Making trouble again?'

'Oh, no,' said Holly. 'No trouble at all.' Her voice was gravelly as ever, but her whiskers were stiff with tension. Above them, the street lamp crackled and fizzed.

Behind Luger, Razor scowled. His face was covered in scars. 'Hanging round with dogs now, are you?' he said, brash and loud. 'Don't you know how wrong that is? It's enough to make you sick!' The rest of the patrol looked at Cludge, and flexed their claws. The big dog blinked.

'Cludge won't hurt you,' said Varjak, trying to sound calm, though his stomach felt tight and his mouth had gone dry.

'Wasn't talking to you,' snapped Razor. His tail flicked cockily in the snow. 'The Boss has taught us how to deal with dogs. Don't try anything, Doggie, or you'll get hurt!'

Cludge was so much bigger – yet Razor seemed so sure of himself. Don't even look at them, Cludge, thought Varjak. We don't want any trouble. We just want them to go away.

Cludge looked down, very still and silent. Snow settled on his coat.

'Good,' said Luger, cool as ice. 'Now, we're searching for a pair of outlaws. Twin cats: one big, one bigger. Have you seen them?'

'No outlaws here,' said Holly. 'We're just talking.'

'You've been hunting!' said Razor. He licked his lips. 'Look, Luger, they've got a mouse. It's ages since we've had mouse.' His tail flicked. 'Give it over. Now.'

Varjak looked at his mouse. Snow swirled through the alley.

'I said, give me that mouse!' repeated Razor. Luger watched with emotionless eyes. Varjak's heart thumped in his throat. He felt dizzy. He was so hungry. He'd been searching all day for this mouse.

'Give him the mouse, Varjak!' whispered Holly.

'Why should I?' The words slipped out of his mouth before he could stop them. He stared down at the snow. He couldn't believe what he'd said.

Razor's ears twitched, like he couldn't believe it either. Then his fur puffed up. His muscles rippled under his stripy coat. 'You'll do it because it's the law!' he growled. 'If you're not in our gang, you can't hunt mice. You have to eat rubbish.'

The wind whipped into Varjak's face. The law? He'd never heard of this law. He was still so new to the city; maybe Holly knew about it. But she looked troubled.

'Wait,' she said. 'That's the law in Sally Bones's territory, on the West side. No one else would hunt there. No one would even go there. But this is the city centre. It's neutral ground, free for all.'

'Not any more,' said Luger.

'What do you mean?' said Holly. 'What about us cats who live in the centre?'

'You will obey the law,' said Luger coldly. 'Anyone who breaks the law will be taken before Sally Bones and punished. Now, Varjak Paw: give Razor that mouse.'

There was no arguing with Luger. He spoke of the law with absolute authority, in a voice as harsh and cold as winter. Even Holly had no answer to him.

Varjak shivered. He surrendered the mouse without a fight, without even a word. He stood there, silent, and let Razor snatch it away from him.

The gang cats gobbled it down. They licked their lips. Then the rusty gate rattled, and Tam came out of the dump, swinging her bushy tail proudly behind her.

'Hey, Varjak, I found something good to eat, buried at the back!' she said, and then she saw the patrol, and her tail curled up. 'L-L-Luger?' she stuttered. 'Razor?'

'Tam!' said Razor. 'Always thinking about food! Aren't you fat enough already?' The gang cats cackled. Tam tried to laugh along with them, but all that came out of her mouth was a strangled-sounding noise.

'Enough!' snapped Luger. The cackling stopped dead. 'This dump belongs to Sally Bones now. If there's anything good to eat in there, it's ours.' He turned to the patrol. 'Uzi, Shane: come with me. Razor: stay here and guard these cats till we come back. Do it properly this time, and perhaps we'll save you a scrap.'

Luger and the others went through the gate. Tam shuddered as they passed her. Razor stood there in

18

the snow, tail swishing furiously behind him.

'Right,' he growled at Varjak and his friends, when the others were gone. 'You three'd better not mess things up for me. Tam, you're in *such* big trouble. You were breaking the law. And you know what happens to law-breakers?' The scars on his face twisted up like snakes. 'They get Sally Bones's punishment.'

Tam flinched at the word. 'Please – no!' she gulped.

Razor leaned in close to her. He ran a claw along the edge of her ear. Tam flinched away – but Razor moved faster. He came in low behind her, and bit her bushy tail, hard.

'Stop it!' shrieked Tam. 'Leave me alone!'

Varjak clenched his paws. He was getting angry. All that talk of the law had confused him, but now he knew what was going on. This was bullying. He'd grown up being bullied by his brother, and he didn't like it one bit. He wanted it to stop.

He caught Cludge's eye, and nodded. The black dog stood up to his full height, and shook the snow from his coat.

'Enough,' Cludge growled at Razor.

Razor turned to face him. All around them, the wind was rising, getting colder.

'I'm not scared of you,' said Razor. 'A pack of

dogs – that's scary. But without a pack, a little Doggie on its own is nothing.'

'Cludge got a pack. Got friends. You leave Cludge's friends alone!'

'Your friends are cats,' jeered Razor, as the snow pelted down around them. 'You should stick with your own kind, you stupid, stinking moron! What's wrong – won't the other Doggies talk to you any more?'

Cludge's black eyes clouded over. He began to quake. He leaned in close to Razor, so his muzzle was just above the tomcat's head – and then he roared a mighty, deafening roar, like thunder.

Varjak grinned. Go on, Cludge, he thought. Razor thinks he's so tough. Let's see how tough he is now!

But Razor stood his ground – and exploded into action. His claws arced up, up, and slashed a vicious curve through Cludge's soft, wet nose.

The big dog howled. He twisted away, turning his face left and right and left, spraying blood into the snow. He stumbled back from Razor's claws, and hid behind Varjak, trembling, whimpering, bleeding from the nose.

It was over.

Varjak's stomach turned liquid. Razor strutted before them, tail held insolently high and proud, fur rippling in triumph. 'Who else wants a fight?' he crowed. 'You. Varjak Paw. You were lucky last time. If the Boss hadn't cut in, I'd have had you. But they never let me forget it – never!' He bared his teeth. 'This time, you're mine.'

And here came Razor. Big. Brawny. Barging towards him through the snow.

No time to think. Only one thing for it: the Way. The fighting Skills.

Fourth Skill: Slow-Time.
Varjak breathed deep,
and counted.

In—two—three—four.

The world seemed to shimmer.

Out–two–three–four.

Everything slowed down.

In–two–three–four.

But Varjak felt fast.

Out–two–three–four.

Power rose up in him.

Now the Fifth Skill: Moving
Circles. He made the power flow
into a circle of pure energy, hot
and strong in the winter night.

27

'Look!' cried Tam. 'Look, he's shimmering!'

'Varjak, no!' warned Holly. 'He'll kill you—'

Wind streaked through Varjak's fur. Snow spiralled down around him. He braced himself, and as Razor sprang through the air, he spun his Moving Circle out to meet him.

SMASH! The impact knocked Varjak off his paws. But the Moving Circle held true. He rolled with the blow. He twisted, turned, and tipped Razor off-balance.

Razor recovered fast. He lashed out with his back legs. Slashed at Varjak's face. It was a fearsome kick, and it connected with brutal accuracy.

Blood spattered on the snow around them. Varjak was cut.

He ignored the stinging pain. Gathered his power. Let the energy rise up in him, let it build – and as Razor came to finish him, he unleashed it in a blinding burst of force.

SLAM!

Razor blinked. His legs gave way. The big cat sank to the ground. Varjak dived in, pinned him, held him down. The energy blazed through him.

SLAM!

    SLAM!

        SLAM!

He pounded Razor, again and again. The power was so strong. It filled his mind. He couldn't stop. I'm going to teach Razor a lesson, he thought. This bully who's hurt my friends and stolen my food – I'm going to smash him up so badly he'll never fight again –

'Varjak!' He heard a gravelly voice, far away. Holly's voice. He stopped hitting Razor, and turned round. Holly was right behind him. 'Varjak, that's enough.'

He looked down at Razor. The tiger-striped tom-cat was gazing up at him, helpless. Dazed, bloodied, he was almost out cold. One more hit and he'd be finished.

Varjak started to shake. What had he done? He'd lost control. Lost it completely.

He dropped his paws. Put away his claws. He stood up, and let Razor go free.

'What?' gasped Razor, blinking. 'Aren't you – aren't you going to—?'

'No,' said Varjak. He was shaking, shaking with the force of it. Holly, Tam and Cludge were looking at him, eyes wide.

'Let's get out of here,' said Holly, 'before Luger and the others get back!'

Chapter Three

Varjak and his friends raced away from the alley. They left the dump behind, and sprinted into the night. New streets opened up ahead of them. Above, the moon shone through clouds.

'You showed him, Varjak!' said Tam. 'Did you see it, Holly? You saw what he did to that big bully?'

'It was crazy!' said Holly. 'It was amazing!' She was smiling; so was Tam.

Varjak tried to smile with them, but he couldn't. He felt scared. He was scared of his power. It had grown so strong, it had taken him over. He might have even killed Razor, if Holly hadn't stopped him.

He came out of Slow-Time. It was hard. The side of his face was starting to throb. That must have been where Razor slashed him.

'What's wrong, Varjak?' said Holly, as they ran through neon streets. 'You won!'

'I went too far.'

'Razor would've done worse,' panted Tam.

'He deserved it,' said Holly. 'He hasn't been the same since he joined that gang.'

Tam's ears twitched. 'What's going to happen when Luger comes back? And when *she* finds out?'

Varjak glanced over his shoulder. For a moment, he thought he could see Sally Bones, the thin white cat, coming after him with her ice-blue eye. But it was just a neon light, flashing through the snow.

'We'll lie low,' said Holly. 'We'll hide for the night. Follow me!'

Varjak followed, glad to have Holly by his side. She always knew what to do. He didn't want to fight any more. He just wanted to hide, to huddle up and go to sleep, somewhere secret, somewhere safe.

They came to a row of tall brick buildings. Between the buildings, there was a maze of narrow passages. Holly plunged into the maze, and led them swiftly through. Snow lay thick on the ground. As they ran, new snow filled in their paw-prints behind them, and covered the trail from Cludge's bloody nose.

'Cludge sorry,' panted the big dog. 'Should of . . . Could of . . .' He tailed off. 'Sorry,' he concluded.

'No, Cludge!' said Tam. 'You were so brave. You stood up for me, and I'll never forget it. Except – maybe you shouldn't stay with us – you'll only get in trouble—'

'Cludge stay! Stay with friends! Always!'

Tam smiled. So did Varjak. But Holly was shaking her head.

'Cludge, you can stay as long as you like,' she said. 'But don't you have a family? Or some friends who are . . . you know . . . dogs?'

Cludge's eyes went cloudy. 'Family?' he muttered. 'Cludge got no family.'

'Why not?'

'Angry with Cludge. Can never go back. Never!'

'Well, there's only one place to hide,' said Holly, 'and you're too big for it. Look.'

Before them now were some black iron railings, deep in the shadows of a back street. The railings were hidden behind heaps of rubble and coils of electrical cable. It looked like a dead end that didn't lead anywhere, but this was actually the entrance to a little network of alleys. Only Varjak, Holly and Tam knew about these secret alleys. They were right in the centre of the city, in the neutral ground that didn't belong to Sally Bones. It was the only safe place they knew, and Varjak had never felt more glad to see it.

hisssssssss!

His neck fur prickled. He heard something in the shadows. It sounded like a cat. A cornered cat, with its back against the wall. And there was the strangest scent: something unnatural, like a cat's ghost.

An animal bolted out of the shadows, into the

night. Varjak hardly saw it; just a blur at the edge of his vision. It was the size of a cat, but it couldn't be a cat. It was the wrong shape. No tail, and its head was . . . he wasn't sure what it was. He turned to look, but it was gone.

'What was that?' he said.

Tam's fur was standing on end, like she'd had an electric shock. 'It's – it's—'

'It's all right,' said Holly. 'It's gone now.'

'But what *was* it?' said Varjak. 'And how could it find the secret alleys? And—'

'It's nothing to do with us. Forget about it. It was hiding in the shadows; it didn't find the alleys.' Holly shimmied past the rubble, through the railings, and disappeared onto the other side. 'It's all clear,' came her voice. 'Everything's safe in here. But you see the problem, Cludge? We're going through these railings. They're too small for a dog.'

Varjak still felt rattled by the strange animal, whatever it was; but it was gone now, and Holly was right about Cludge. He could see she was right – yet he could also see Cludge, pressing his muzzle into the railings, trying to follow, trying to fit.

'Then . . .' panted Cludge, 'then . . . Cludge guard it!' He moved in front of the railings, covering them with his huge body, and made his most fearsome face. 'Cludge not scared!' He snapped his teeth. 'Cludge guarding!'

'Oh, Cludge,' said Tam. 'He can stay, can't he, Varjak?'

'It's dangerous!' came Holly's voice. 'We can't leave him out there, like a giant signpost—'

'He's our friend,' said Varjak, 'and he's staying if he wants to.' He turned to the big dog. 'You stay here, Cludge. Stay and guard it. Bark if anyone bad comes.'

Cludge barked and wagged his tail, sending up a flurry of snow. Tam cheered.

'It's asking for trouble,' said Holly, 'but there's no time to argue. Now get in here, before Sally Bones comes!'

Varjak and Tam scrambled through the railings, into the secret alleys.

There were no neon lights here; just the faintest glow from faraway windows. Fire escapes led up to the rooftops. Drainpipes snaked down, through grilles in the ground, to sewers below. The ground was made of tight-packed cobblestones. The alleys were sheltered from the weather, so the cobbles were dry and free from snow. A little warmth filtered up from the sewers through those grilles in the ground. Varjak could see something glimmering down there, like water moving far beneath the frozen city.

He curled up in a corner. 'It's good to be back,' he sighed.

'I'm never leaving the secret alleys again,' said Tam, as she made herself comfortable.

'Then you'll never eat another mouse,' said Holly. 'Except in your dreams.'

'Mmm . . .' she murmured. 'Sweet, sweet dreams.'

'Shame we lost that mouse,' mused Holly. 'I wish we'd eaten it before they got there. But then we would've had Sally Bones's punishment—'

'What is Sally Bones's punishment, anyway?' said Varjak.

'You don't want to know,' said Holly. 'There shouldn't be a punishment, should there? All cats should be allowed to hunt, not just her gang.'

'I'm never hunting again,' muttered Tam. 'Not after tonight. And not when she does those horrible things—'

'What things?' said Varjak. Tam just flinched.

Holly's ears and tail twitched. 'Don't say. It's too horrible.' She shook her head. 'You know what gets me most?' she said, changing the subject. 'It's the way they call it *the law*, as if it's something we all agree on. But it's not. They just do whatever they want, and we have to accept it.'

'And now we can't even go to the dump any more!' groaned Tam. 'If we don't get some food soon, I'll waste away! I'll become thin!'

'What gives them the right?' said Holly. 'Just because they're bigger and stronger than us, they think they can push us around.' There was silence for a moment. Then she carried on, very quietly, her voice full of gravel. 'We shouldn't be scared of them,' she said. 'So many cats in this city hate the Bones gang. Mrs Moggs always says we should stand up to them, but no one ever dares.'

'Mrs Moggs?' said Varjak.

'The oldest, wisest cat in the city,' said Tam. 'She lives by the river, in the centre, where we grew up. Wait till she hears how you beat Razor! We'll take you to meet her tomorrow – right, Holly?'

Holly yawned. 'Maybe. Right now, though, we could all use some sleep.' She curled up in the shadows, next to Tam. 'Night, Varjak,' she said, as her eyes closed.

Varjak frowned. He'd always dreamed of being a

great fighter, the greatest – but reality was turning out to be more difficult than any dream. *Wait till she hears how you beat Razor.* He didn't even want to think about how he'd lost control of his power, or about Luger and Sally Bones, and that strange animal he'd seen outside the secret alleys . . .

He was too tired to think at all. He shut his eyes. A great wave of exhaustion washed over him, and took him down into sleep.

Chapter Four

Varjak dreamed.

He dreamed he was standing on a mountain at sunrise. The air tasted sharp and sweet, like wild mint. Everything seemed brighter and clearer than normal. Everything was glowing with silent sunlight. The sky was so clear and blue, he could see the stars, though it was daytime.

An old cat stood beside him. He wasn't big, but something about him looked dangerous. His fur was silver-blue and his eyes were amber, like Varjak's. It was Jalal: Varjak's ancestor, who he met in dreams, and who'd taught him the Way.

'Where are we, Jalal?' said Varjak.

'The mountains of Mesopotamia,' said Jalal. 'We are on top of the world. Everything starts here.'

He gestured at a silver stream, shimmering beneath them in the sun. The stream flowed down into a river that wound through hills and valleys below, making the world green with life. On the banks of the river, far away, sparkled a city.

'You were down there when last we met,' said Jalal. 'Down on the ground with everyone else. But now see where you are?'

Varjak looked around. They were completely alone on top of the mountain. The blueness of the sky was dazzling, the silence pressed in on his ears, and the wild mint air was making him light-headed. They were too high; higher than the sun.

'What am I doing here, Jalal?' he said. 'I know

the Seven Skills, I know everything you've taught me, and here I am, on the highest mountain—'

'The highest mountain?' interrupted Jalal, eyes sparkling with amusement. 'Well. Perhaps you are here because you have more to learn. When first you came to Mesopotamia, you were but a helpless kitten.'

'I didn't know anything back then. I thought I wanted to be a great fighter.'

'And you no longer wish that?' said Jalal. 'That is good. For truly great fighters know there are things more powerful than fighting. Seeing, for instance.'

'I don't want to be a fighter!' snapped Varjak. The old cat just looked at him calmly. 'Anyway, seeing's not powerful,' he muttered. 'Everyone knows how to see.'

'Yes?' said Jalal. 'You know how to see, and yet you say you are on the highest mountain?'

Varjak looked down. He saw the hills and valleys below. He looked up, and saw the sky, with stars as clear as day. No mountains above him; only sky.

'That's right,' he said. 'The highest mountain.'

'Hmm,' said Jalal. 'You have much to learn, indeed. Now see what is behind you.'

Varjak turned round – and what he saw, he would never forget.

A whole range of mountains reared up above him. They were impossibly huge and white. Their sheer faces filled the sky: massive, unknowable, a perfect mystery. And he was only on the lowest peak.

'There are more mountains beyond those too,' chuckled Jalal, 'and more, even higher, on the other side. Look in the wrong direction, and you would never notice them. But up in those mountains, perhaps you will learn what is more powerful than fighting. So come now, Varjak Paw. Come climb with me.'

Chapter Five

Varjak woke in the secret alleys. It was late afternoon. The first street lights were flickering on. High above, a few bright windows lit up the dark outlines of city buildings. The snow had stopped, but it was still freezing cold, and the wind chilled him beneath his fur. He huddled by one of those grilles in the ground, beside a drainpipe. It didn't smell good, but at least it was warm.

Holly and Tam were already up. They'd been searching the secret alleys for food. They hadn't found a thing.

'Where do all the mice go in winter?' sighed Holly. 'I wish I knew. Maybe Mrs Moggs'll have some. You ready to go, Varjak?'

He nodded. He felt better after sleeping, and he was hungry again. But Tam looked worried. She was crouched in a corner, by a fire escape, nibbling nervously at her paws.

'We're not going now, are we?' she said. 'I

dreamed of the white cat last night . . .'

'What, Sally Bones?' said Holly.

'Ssh! Don't say her name! She'll hear you! And then she'll—'

'Tam, calm down,' said Holly. 'It's OK.'

'It's not OK! She'll be looking for us, after last night.'

'Well, we can't hide here for ever. We've got to eat. And Mrs Moggs always has something good to eat.'

Tam bit her fur. 'I'm not hungry.'

'Now that's a first,' grinned Holly. She leaned in close to Tam, and whispered temptingly. 'Think of the mice. The taste of fresh mice—'

'Too risky.'

'Hot, juicy mice—'

Tam licked her lips. 'Stop it,' she pleaded.

'Melting in your mouth—'

'No! I said stop it, Holly, and I meant it! I'm not going out. It'll be night soon, and *she'll* be on the prowl.'

'Fine,' said Holly. 'Stay here on your own. Come on, Varjak.'

She slipped out through the railings. Tam gawped.

'Come on, Tam,' said Varjak. He knew it was risky, but he was going with Holly. He couldn't imagine being in the city without her. Besides, he wanted to meet Mrs Moggs.

He emerged from the secret alleys into the winter afternoon. Cludge was squatting in the rubble, guarding the railings. He barked cheerily at them.

'Where you go?' he asked.

'We're meeting some cats in town,' said Holly.

'Cats?' He blinked. 'Cludge come?'

Holly frowned. 'Of course you can come. Only – you'll scare them. It's just that – well, you're a dog, Cludge, and we're cats.'

Varjak could see her point. He didn't like it, though. He hated the idea of leaving Cludge on his own.

But Cludge seemed relieved. 'Cludge not meet cats,' he said. 'Cludge stay.' He planted himself firmly down in the rubble again. It looked like nothing would ever shift him from the spot. 'Tam not go?' he panted.

'No, she's too scared,' said Holly.

'Silly Tam!' barked Cludge.

'Yes, she's a very silly Tam,' said Holly, loudly. 'And she's going to be a hungry Tam, too, because we won't be bringing any food back for her – no juicy mice, no scrumptious fish – nothing!'

Tam squeezed out through the railings. 'All right, all right, I'm coming!' she said. 'But only because I'm a greedy, stupid Tam!'

They all laughed, and the three cats set off into the city. Just for a moment, Varjak thought he saw a flash of winter sun through the clouds, lighting up the sky, but then the clouds closed, and it darkened quickly. It was late afternoon, so there were many people about, bustling and striding along the pavements. The main roads were full of screeching, roaring cars.

The three friends avoided them, and stuck to alleys where these noises faded, and it was quiet enough to hear their own paws, padding through the snow. This was the world of cats: invisible to people, but going on constantly, just below the city's surface.

There were many walls before them. Holly always found a way over. She led them up lofty ledges, along strips of scaffolding, and down the other side. Varjak loved climbing walls. It felt free, up in the air, off the ground. This is how it should be, he thought to himself. The city's a magical, wonderful place. It's our place. And now we're going to meet some new friends.

But as night fell on the city, even Holly looked nervous. They came to a wall with clusters of barbed wire along the top, and thick metal bars. It was scarred with holes. Posters were peeling off it; graffiti was sprayed all over.

They climbed up carefully and tiptoed forwards, avoiding the wire, keeping their balance on the edge. One mis-step and they'd fall, or be ripped to pieces by the barbs.

Varjak's Awareness tingled with danger. At first,

he thought it was because of the wire. Then he wondered: was someone following them?

His fur prickled up. He focused on the sounds. And there, beneath the rumble of the city, he heard paws, padding behind them.

They were being followed. Whoever it was couldn't be friendly, or they would've said something by now. Varjak's happy thoughts vanished, like the sun behind clouds. The city wasn't magical; it was dangerous. You had to fight to survive here.

'There's someone behind us!' he whispered, and whirled around. Holly and Tam turned with him.

Facing them, on top of the wall in the moonlight, Varjak saw three cats he'd never seen before. Tall, thin Siamese cats, with tawny fur and pale green eyes. Their claws were long and curved. They looked lethal.

'It's the Scratch Sisters!' whispered Holly. 'Good fighters—'

'The best fighters in the world!' declared the leanest, meanest, tallest of them all. 'I'm Elyza Scratch. These are my Sisters, Malisha and Pernisha. Who are you?'

'I'm Holly – we've met before.'

'Holly?' said Elyza Scratch. 'Yes, I recognize you now, and your fat friend Tam. But who's that funny-looking little cat with you? You there: what's your name?'

Varjak didn't know what to say. Who were these cats? He could tell they weren't Holly's friends; it was best to be careful. 'I'm new in the city,' he said.

'New?' said Elyza. 'Where do you come from, then?'

'Mesopotamia,' he said brightly.

The Scratch Sisters stared at him, eyes narrow, fur flattening in the wind.

'Mesopo-what?' said Elyza.

'Messuppa-who?' said Malisha.

'Messed-up-wherever,' said Pernisha. 'He's obviously not from round here, is he? He looks like trouble. Just look at that cut on his cheek!'

Varjak tried to smile. 'Oh, that's nothing,' he said. 'I just – er – fell down some stairs.'

'He's lying,' snapped Elyza, polishing her claws on barbed wire.

'He's a cocky little so-and-so,' said Malisha.

Pernisha flashed her claws at Varjak. 'You disrespecting the Scratch Sisters? You think we're stupid? Get off this wall – you don't belong here!'

Varjak's heart jumped. He hadn't meant to, but he'd made them angry. He looked around for a way out. There wasn't one. He was balanced finely on the wall. On one side was barbed wire; on the other, a long, long fall.

Elyza's tail thudded slowly. 'Well? What you waiting for? We're the fastest claws in town – and

49

we never, ever back down.'

'Never!' said Malisha.

'Ever!' said Pernisha.

The three Siamese knifed towards him, ghosting past barbed wire and bars as if they weren't even there.

'Take it easy!' yelled Holly. 'Varjak's my friend – he's OK! He got that cut fighting Razor!'

The Scratch Sisters stopped, just a whisker away from Varjak's face. He could feel their eyes on him, like points of pale green fire.

'Varjak?' said Elyza at last. '*You're* Varjak Paw?'

'We've heard about you,' said Malisha.

'They say you fight like the Bones,' said Pernisha. 'Try it. Go on, just try it, and we'll cut your throat!'

Varjak's pulse was racing. This was becoming a nightmare. He wasn't going to fight them, not after what happened with Razor. There had to be some other way to deal with these fierce, proud cats – but what?

He held up his paws very slowly. 'You're right,' he said. 'It's true I can fight like Sally Bones. But that wouldn't be enough against the Scratch Sisters. No way. You're too powerful. I wouldn't stand a chance against you. No one would.'

The Scratch Sisters blinked, surprised. The fire left their eyes.

'Hmm,' purred Elyza. 'Maybe he's not so bad, after all.'

'He knows what's what,' said Malisha, grooming her tawny fur.

'I still say he's cheeky,' said Pernisha. 'But he's got a bit of respect. Not like *her*.'

'No. He's not like *her*.' Elyza nodded gravely. 'OK: we'll let you live, Paw. But if it's true you fight like the Bones, you better watch out. She's been hunting down the toughest cats in town, and beating them one by one. There's only a few of us left; her gang's taken almost all the city. It's not like the old days any more. Watch your back.'

And with those words, the Scratch Sisters were gone. Faster than Varjak could see, they jack-knifed down from the wall, and ghosted into the evening, tails held high.

Chapter Six

Tam turned to Varjak, wonder in her eyes. 'You made the Scratch Sisters back down!'

'It was me who backed down,' said Varjak. 'I didn't want to fight them.'

'You did the right thing,' said Holly. 'We don't want them as enemies. Now let's get out of here, before someone *really* bad comes!'

She led them down the wall, into the snowy evening. They headed to the river that flowed through the city. Varjak smelled the river before he saw it; he could almost taste the fresh fish. There was a harbour on the river, with boats coming in to dock. Flags fluttered on their masts. Their horns rang out loud, and lights played on the water. Seagulls wheeled and turned above.

'Smell that lovely fish?' said Tam, licking her chops. 'It's Mrs Moggs's favourite!'

A row of brown buildings faced the harbour, coated in snow like everything else. A flight of steps ran down between the buildings, to a yard at the bottom. Though bounded by buildings, the yard was open to the sky, with fire escapes zigzagging up. Lights were on in many windows, casting a warm glow. It was a cosy-looking place, but Varjak couldn't help noticing the fire escapes were the only way out, apart from the steps they'd come in by.

The yard was bustling with cats. Not gang cats, just ordinary street cats: long-haired and short-haired, large and small, all different colours and types. Some of them were nosing around a heap of old packing crates in the corner of the yard. Others were clustered together, grooming each other's fur, gossiping and chattering. A few were lapping at pools of ice on the ground, trying to get at the water below.

Varjak looked closer. There didn't seem to be any food here. Though these cats looked cheerful, they were all much thinner than Sally Bones's gang. They lacked the big, brawny muscles of those who ran the city.

In the centre of the yard, beside a ship's anchor and a heap of chain, an old marmalade tabby was telling some kittens a story.

'It's the most wonderful place,' she was saying, her bright blue eyes gleaming. 'It's always warm, and there's more mice than you can eat.'

'But if it's so wonderful, Grandma,' said a

marmalade kitten in the crowd, 'why don't we go there right now?'

The old tabby combed her long whiskers. 'Well, it's not easy to get there, Jessie. It's protected by fearsome guardians, and there's the most disgusting smell you can imagine, so most cats don't even know about it! But we sheltered there, years ago, when I was just your age. There was a great fire in the city, see, and we had to hide . . .'

Above the yard, seagulls rose up on the river breeze. Harbour lights winked into the night.

'That's Mrs Moggs,' whispered Holly, but Varjak had guessed as soon as he saw her. 'She told us that tale when we were kittens. Remember, Tam?'

'I remember! If only it was true.'

Mrs Moggs looked up at the steps, alert despite her years. 'But it *is* true, young Tammie, my dear,' she said. 'Every word.'

'I – I didn't mean it wasn't—'

'Tam!' cried the marmalade kitten. 'And Holly!' She bounded out to meet them on the steps. 'Look, everyone – they're back! The Vanishings didn't get them, after all!'

A buzz went round the yard. The street cats stopped doing what they were doing and looked over, their ears and tails perking up with excitement.

'Well, now,' said Mrs Moggs, as Jess led the three of them down to the anchor in the centre of the yard. 'Holly and Tam, it's mighty good to see you two again! We was so worried about you. But who's this with you?'

'He's my friend,' said Holly. 'His name's Varjak Paw. He's the one who saved us from the Vanishings. It's thanks to him they're all over now.'

The buzz of interest intensified. The street cats were smiling and purring at Varjak, welcoming him to the harbour yard. They were so different to Sally Bones's gang or the Scratch Sisters; so open and friendly. Already, he felt at home here.

'I'm Jess,' said the marmalade kitten. 'And if you're the cat who solved the Vanishings, we should give you a welcome feast, like a hero!'

The street cats all nodded at that, murmuring happily and licking their lips – all except one of them. A skinny old cat with a sour look on his face, like he'd eaten something rotten.

'Solved the Vanishings?' he sniffed, peering at Varjak. 'He don't look big enough—'

'Who cares how big he is?' said Jess. 'Just ignore Old Buckley, Varjak. He's a horrible grump!'

Varjak didn't mind; he was enjoying himself. 'Well, Old Buckley's right. I couldn't have done it without Holly and Tam, and our friend Cludge. And it's great to meet you all!'

'What a nice young cat,' purred Mrs Moggs. 'I like your friend, Holly.'

'He's *my* friend too!' piped up Tam. Everyone laughed. In the harbour, a ship's horn sang out into the night, rich and brassy. The yard was bathed in warm sounds. 'And guess what else?' said Tam, encouraged. 'Varjak's been standing up to *her* gang. He fought Razor – and beat him!' A gasp went round the yard.

Varjak shook his head. 'Tam – don't—'

But little Jess was looking at him with her bright blue eyes like no one had ever looked at him before. There was a kind of faith there that made his scalp tingle.

'You beat that mean old Razor?' she said. 'Grandma's always saying someone should stand up to the Bones gang! If I was bigger—'

'Don't get your hopes up!' said Old Buckley. 'He don't look like no fighter to me.'

'Varjak *is* a fighter,' insisted Tam. 'A great fighter.'

'I'm not,' said Varjak. 'It's not true. I don't want to fight anyone.'

'Why do you think the Scratch Sisters backed down?' said Tam. 'They could tell—'

'Them cats never back down!' breathed Jess. 'I wish you'd stick around, Varjak – we could use your help.'

'Stick around?' spluttered Old Buckley. '*Him?* Think about it, Jessie! If he really beat Razor, they'll

58

come looking for him. Haven't we got enough trouble as it is? I wish he'd get out of here and leave us alone!'

Mrs Moggs shook her head. 'Sometimes I wonder about you lot,' she said. 'Jessie, that's enough talk about fighting. Varjak's our guest. We don't ask guests to get into fights on our behalf. And we certainly don't insult them, Buckley!'

'Pff,' sniffed Old Buckley. 'I wasn't insulting no one. Just speaking my mind.'

'I'm sorry about him, my dears,' said Mrs Moggs. 'He's scared, that's all. You can't blame him. It's unnatural, what's happening in this city. We've seen things we never thought we'd see.'

'It's all right,' said Varjak. 'I know what you mean. We saw something strange last night – didn't we, Holly? It was like some kind of cat, only it didn't have a tail, and its head was the wrong shape—'

He stopped talking, for the atmosphere had shifted again. Suddenly, no one was laughing any more, or purring, or even moving. Everyone was looking down at the ground. An uncomfortable silence fell on the yard. Mrs Moggs shook her head.

'Strange days indeed,' she said. 'I wish we could welcome you properly. I'd put on a good old-fashioned feast for you, like Jessie said – only we got no food.'

Tam's face fell. 'No food? Really? But – I thought

– how can you have no food?'

Mrs Moggs sighed. 'This winter's so hard already, see, there's precious little to go round as it is, and now them Bones cats are taking what we got, and calling it the law. The fish from the harbour, that lovely fresh fish you can smell? They come every night and take it from us. Anyone what says different – well, we know what happens to them. *Sally Bones's punishment.*'

The silence deepened. Varjak scratched his head. He was probably the only one who didn't know what Sally Bones's punishment was. Maybe Mrs Moggs would tell him – but Jess spoke up again before he could ask.

'What was Sally Bones like, Grandma? Before she beat all them other gangs, and took over the city?'

Mrs Moggs dropped into a conspiratorial whisper. 'No one knows. The Bones weren't always in this city, see. They say she came out of the North, and she's been wandering the earth for a hundred years, changing her name wherever she goes—'

Old Buckley laughed out loud. 'Tales!'

'– and have you noticed?' Mrs Moggs carried on. 'You only ever see her at night. It's because she'd burn up in daylight, she's that evil!'

'That's the stupidest tale I ever heard!' scoffed Buckley. 'Sally Bones is evil, all right, but she's just a cat – no different to you or me. But next, Old

Moggs'll be telling you there's a secret city, what no one else knows about—'

'There is!' she cried. 'I was just saying!'

'And I always believed you,' said Holly. 'But if it's true – then where is this city?'

'Well now,' said Mrs Moggs. She drew back and took a deep breath, like she was about to tell another tale. But before she could, a pair of kittens came barrelling down the steps into the yard. They were out of breath; their eyes were round with fear.

'What is it?' said Mrs Moggs.

'It's *them*! The Bones gang! Luger and that lot – they're in the harbour!'

Panic ripped through the yard like winter wind. Varjak looked up the steps, and saw them coming. Ten of them or more. This was no ordinary patrol. It was a deadly fighting force from Sally Bones's gang.

A claw of panic cut into his guts. Cold fear spilled out, flooding his body. Jess was looking at him, eyes glowing. She thought he was a hero. She thought he could take them on and win. She was wrong. His power wouldn't be enough against all those cats. The Way couldn't help him; it only brought trouble.

'You'd better hide, my dear,' said Mrs Moggs gently. 'It's you they'll be after.'

Varjak nodded; he couldn't speak. His legs felt heavy, his head felt light.

'Let's use the fire escapes!' said Holly.

'Too late,' said Mrs Moggs. 'They'll see you, and chase you, and it'll be worse. No, you better hide, and fast.'

'But where?' choked Tam. 'Oh, we should never have come, Holly, I told you—'

'Them crates in the corner,' said Mrs Moggs. 'Do it now!'

Crates? Varjak didn't understand – but Holly did. She dragged him and Tam over to the pile of old packing crates in the corner of the yard. The crates were discarded, broken, covered in snow. One of them had a crack just wide enough for a cat to slip through, so they nosed into it, and huddled together in the dark.

They could hear Mrs Moggs, calling out to the street cats in the yard. 'Now don't panic! We done nothing wrong. Let's face them with dignity, for once.'

But the panic was contagious. It swept through them all like a storm. As he hid in the crate with his friends, Varjak's heart hammered in his chest. Tam shivered beside him. Even Holly was silent.

Because through the crack, he could see them coming down the steps. The roughest, toughest cats in town – and it looked like they meant business.

Chapter Seven

It was dark in the crate. It was full of buzzing flies and it smelled of rotten fruit. The ground was slimy-sticky under Varjak's paws.

He peered out through the crack, heart pounding. Sally Bones's cats were stalking down the steps. They walked in line, a tight disciplined line, each guarding the others. They looked so much bigger and stronger than the street cats. They looked very well fed.

They were led by Luger, the grey cat with emotionless eyes. Behind him came Razor, strutting tall as ever, despite the fight. After Razor came Uzi and Shane and six others. Each one was terrifying. The street cats cowered away from them, and clustered round Mrs Moggs, by the anchor.

'We're looking for a cat called Varjak Paw,' snapped out Luger, cold as ice. 'He's new in town. Who knows where he is?'

Varjak's heart lurched. One word, one look,

could give him away. But the street cats didn't say a thing. They didn't even glance at the crates.

'This cat is small but dangerous,' said Luger. 'He's an outsider, not from round here. He doesn't respect our laws. He was hunting mice in the city dump, which belongs to our gang. Then he attacked one of us, totally unprovoked. Isn't that right, Razor?'

Razor's tail swished behind him. 'That's right.'

'Sally Bones wants him, dead or alive,' said Luger. 'He's an outlaw, and so are his friends Holly and Tam. We know they're your friends too. Where are they?'

Varjak's insides felt like liquid. Outlaw? Dead or alive? How had this happened?

Out in the yard, Mrs Moggs spoke up. 'Well now, Luger,' she said, quiet but firm. 'First of all, I do believe the dump is part of the city centre. It's neutral ground. It don't belong to your gang.'

Luger didn't blink. 'And what else?' he said.

'Second,' said Mrs Moggs, 'we don't know this Parjak Vaw, or whatever he's called.' Her words crack-led round the yard like electricity. Luger shook his head.

'That's a shame,' he said. 'Because Sally Bones is offering a reward for information. Fresh fish and juicy mice, as much as you can eat.'

Varjak's heart twisted inside his chest. Luger had offered them the one thing they all wanted. But everyone stayed silent; even Old Buckley. They just looked down at the ground. Above, a seagull squawked a long, hoarse cry into the night.

'Let me say it again,' said Luger, 'so there's no doubt. Varjak Paw is an outlaw. We will find him, we will hunt him down, and we will bring him to justice. The same goes for anyone who helps him or hides him. They will be hunted down in the same way, and taken before Sally Bones for punishment. Do you understand?'

As Varjak listened, an insect buzzed in his ear. It landed on his nose. He could feel its legs, crawling on his face. But there was nothing he could do. Sally Bones's gang would hear him if he made a sound. *Keep still. Don't move. Don't even breathe.*

Out in the yard, there was silence, a roaring silence.

Luger nodded at his lieutenants, beside him. 'Uzi. Shane. Do your thing.'

Uzi and Shane grinned. They stalked around the yard, tails flicking with menace. They pushed and prodded the street cats. Varjak could see the street cats' fur rising with fear; their little huddles breaking up. He felt the fear himself, rising in his guts.

'It's going to get worse,' said Luger, 'if you don't tell us what we want to know.'

'Call your thugs off,' said Mrs Moggs. 'We don't know nothing.'

Luger sidled up to her. 'Is that so?' he hissed.

Varjak's stomach knotted as he watched – but Mrs Moggs didn't flinch. 'Yes it is,' she said simply. 'And I'll tell you what else, now you ask. Them fish and mice you're offering as reward? They belong to us anyway. You stole them from us.'

Luger stared at Mrs Moggs. She looked straight back at him, dignified and calm. Luger blinked first. He shook his head with irritation, and snuck around behind her.

'And who's this?' he said, dragging out the marmalade-coloured kitten.

'It's little Jess!' said Razor. He strutted over. Jess tried to back away, but Luger held her there. The knots in Varjak's stomach tightened.

'Don't you hurt my Jessie,' said Mrs Moggs, her fur beginning to rise. 'Don't you hurt her, you hear me?'

'We wouldn't dream of it!' said Razor, big and loud. 'We don't want to hurt anyone. We just want to protect you from a dangerous outlaw. You understand that, don't you, Jess? Now why don't you save everyone a lot of trouble, and tell us where to find Varjak Paw and his friends, eh?'

'I d-don't know,' said Jess in a wavery voice.

Luger shoved Razor aside, and unsheathed his claws in front of Jess's face. 'You're a pretty little kitten,' he said, cold as ice. 'You want to stay pretty,

don't you? You don't want to end up with nasty scars everywhere, like Razor here. *Now tell us where he is.*'

Jess stood there, trembling. So did Varjak, in the crate, and Holly and Tam beside him. He felt helpless. Totally helpless.

'Have a heart, Luger,' pleaded Mrs Moggs. 'Jessie's only little.'

Luger laughed. Varjak saw him look at Razor, a question in his eyes. Razor shivered, hesitated a moment – and then nodded.

'Right,' said Luger to the crowd. 'If you don't tell us what we want to know, this kitten will be punished.'

A spasm of horror ran through the yard. Luger seized Jess by the scruff. She twisted and turned, but it was no good. He had her, and he was dragging her away.

'No!' cried Mrs Moggs. 'Not my Jessie!' She reached for her granddaughter – but the other gang cats shoved her back. They flashed their deadly claws and teeth at the crowd, keeping them at bay.

'We'll give you a chance,' said Razor. 'You've got till tomorrow night. If no one talks by then – you'll have to deal with Sally Bones herself.'

The street cats recoiled at her name. They shrank back in terror, sinking into the snow. Razor, Luger and the rest of them strode up the steps, out of the yard, dragging Jess away. She was writhing, Mrs Moggs was howling, but no one lifted a paw to stop it happening. There was no resistance. No one dared.

Chapter Eight

In the crate, Varjak's heart was pounding. Sally Bones's gang had left the yard, but Jess was gone, Mrs Moggs was sobbing, and it was all because of him.

'Can't believe it,' he whispered. 'She's only a kitten. How could they do that?'

'I know,' said Holly.

They sat in silence a while, in the darkness of the crate, with the smell of rotting fruit and the buzzing of the flies.

'I'll miss Jessie,' said Tam. 'She was lovely. I remember when she was born—'

'You're talking about her like she's dead,' said Holly.

'It'd be better if she *was* dead. You know what they'll do to her. We're just lucky they didn't find us.'

'The only reason they didn't find us,' said Holly, 'is because Jess didn't give us away.' She gave Varjak a long, hard look, her mustard eyes glowing fierce in the dark.

Varjak looked down. He hadn't wanted trouble, but trouble had found him anyway. The cats of the harbour yard had welcomed him, treated him like a hero. They'd stood up for him. And now Jess was gone – and he hadn't lifted a paw to stop it.

He felt ashamed.

I can't let this happen, he thought.

But what can I do?

Something stirred inside him. Something old and strong, and buried deep.

His power. Deep inside him, like a spark waiting to be struck, the power was waiting. He didn't want to use it. He was scared to use it. But what choice did he have?

He took a deep breath. 'I know why Jessie stood up for us,' he said. 'Tam, you told her I was a fighter. She believed you. She believed that if we escaped, we'd come back to help her.'

'Help her?' squealed Tam. 'How? They've declared us outlaws! They'll be searching for us everywhere! And they've taken Jess to her territory – *her territory*, Varjak!'

Her words made him shake. He remembered Sally Bones's ice-blue eye, burning into his mind. The thin white cat who also knew the Way. 'I know. I know. And I wouldn't ask either of you to come with me. But I – I've got to do something. I couldn't live with myself if I didn't.' He tried to smile, to hold down the thrumming panic that clawed at his heart. 'I'm going to follow them. I'm going to try and rescue her.'

'Well,' said Holly, 'we can't let him blunder in there on his own, can we, Tam?' Varjak looked up, hardly able to believe it. Holly winked at him. But Tam's tail was thumping behind her, thwacking the sides of the crate with alarm.

'Have you gone completely mad?' she cried. 'No one goes there if they can help it – no one!'

'Tonight, it was Jess,' said Holly evenly. 'Tomorrow, it could be you. Should we just forget about you, and let them take you away, next time?'

'No, of course not, but—'

'But what? In the end, they'll come for us all.'

Varjak wasn't shaking any more. Holly was coming with him. She understood. She always did.

Tam gritted her teeth. 'Oh, I hate you, Holly! I hate you both! I don't know who's worse – you're as mad as each other!'

'Right,' said Holly. 'So here's the plan. If we go after them now, they'll be on their guard. Better if we surprise them. I say we set out at dawn and follow their tracks. If we're lucky, we'll catch them sleeping, and maybe – just maybe – we'll have a chance of getting Jess out alive. Agreed?'

'Agreed,' said Varjak. 'Tam?'

Tam bit her paws. 'Of all the stupid things you've

ever made me do,' she muttered, 'this is the all-time stupidest. It's totally insane. But you're not leaving me here on my own – oh no, no way! So fine. Whatever you say. Agreed!'

Varjak grinned. It was good to have his friends beside him. Whatever happened, he knew he could count on them.

They came out of the crate, into the open. It was freezing cold in the yard. The wind cut through his fur.

The terror was still palpable on the air. He could smell it. The street cats were scared of Luger, Razor and the rest – but the threat of Sally Bones had terrified them most. They were strung out, broken up, defeated. Many of them had slumped to the ground in despair. A few were trying to comfort Mrs Moggs. Varjak took a deep breath, and went straight up to her.

'What do you want now?' demanded Old Buckley. 'Hasn't there been enough trouble?'

'I'm sorry,' he said quietly.

'Some fighter you turned out to be,' sniffed Buckley. 'All that big talk—'

'There was ten of them!' Mrs Moggs cut in. Her whiskery face was crumpled and wet, but her eyes were still bright blue. 'No one could've stood up to them. It's not Varjak's fault. There's nothing anyone can do.'

'Yes, there is,' said Varjak. 'We're going to bring her back.'

They didn't answer. They stared at him as if he'd spoken in another language. 'We're going to bring her back,' he repeated.

'Don't talk rubbish,' hissed Old Buckley. 'She's gone where no one can help her, and that's that.' The wind howled through the harbour.

Varjak shook his head. 'We can do it,' he said. 'We're going at dawn. We're going to bring her back where she belongs.'

'You don't understand, my dear,' said Mrs Moggs, whiskers trembling in the wind. 'They've taken her to Sally Bones's territory. No one comes back from there.'

For a moment, the street cats stared at Varjak, eyes glowing with uncertainty. Then they turned away. They went back to the pools of ice on the ground, and the broken packing crates. No one spoke to him any more, or even glanced at him.

He looked up to the darkening sky. It was going to be a long, cold night.

'Let's get some rest,' said Holly. 'We're going to need it.'

She shut her mustard-coloured eyes, and curled up into a spiky ball. Varjak and Tam curled up beside her, and waited for the dawn.

Chapter Nine

Varjak dreamed that night.

He dreamed he was back in Mesopotamia. He tasted the wild mint air; he blinked in the bright, silent sunlight. The sky was so clear and blue, he could see the stars, even though it was daytime.

He was on the mountain with Jalal. They were standing on the summit. It was a sheer precipice, an open drop: they could walk no further without falling. Yet above them, ahead of them, was that mountain range, impossibly huge and perfect – and impossibly far away.

'Are you ready to climb those mountains?' said Jalal.

'How?' said Varjak. 'We can't climb any further.'

'Sometimes,' said Jalal, 'in order to go up, you must go down.'

Varjak looked down into whiteness. At first, he thought he was staring at the snowy slopes of the nearest mountain. But then the whiteness opened up and drifted away, and he realized with a horrible jolt that he'd actually been looking at a bank of clouds. He was so high, he was higher than the clouds. He felt giddy.

'We can't go down there,' he said. 'It's too far.'

'A single jump should do it,' said Jalal cheerfully.

'But we'll fall!'

'Precisely. We need only fall, and we will be there.'

Varjak looked through the clouds, and saw that the nearest mountain slopes were much further below than he'd thought. He couldn't be sure where space ended and the mountain began. He felt dizzy thinking about it. The view wobbled dangerously, and he had to look up.

'It's too far, Jalal! We'll never make it!'

Jalal drew back. His amber eyes sparkled in the sun. He raised a paw in readiness. Then he raced at the precipice, the drop, the edge of the mountain: and sprang forwards into space.

'Jalal – no!' cried Varjak. He rushed to the edge, just in time to see the old cat arcing through the air, plunging into the clouds – and disappearing from view.

He was gone. Gone. Varjak stood alone on top of the mountain.

He shook his head. This was madness. He couldn't

jump off a mountain! He'd be killed, his body would smash to pieces, he'd surely die –

Yet Jalal had done it.

He looked down. His stomach churned. He didn't like being alone here. The wild mint air was going to his head again. He cursed his mad old ancestor.

But what else could he do? Jalal left him no choice.

He drew back. Shut his eyes. And still cursing the name of Jalal, Varjak Paw ran at the edge of the mountain.

He sprang forwards, and flew into the clearest, bluest sky. Whooping, shrieking, soaring, he plunged through clouds. Air rushed through his fur, his whiskers, his face. He was falling, falling, falling through space, and –

whump!

– finally landing, lightly on his paws, safe on the other side.

He'd done it! He'd crossed the chasm, he'd jumped the void. He'd made it to the other mountain.

Jalal stood beside him, combing his whiskers.

'Not so hard once you let go, is it?' said the old cat. He gestured at a path, winding up into the heights ahead of them. 'And now we have fallen, we can climb once again.'

Chapter Ten

Varjak woke before dawn. It was cold and grey in the harbour yard. Someone was poking him in the ribs. He opened his eyes and saw Holly. Around the yard, the street cats were asleep.

'Come on,' Holly whispered. 'Enough dreaming. Time for action.'

She strode up the steps. Varjak and Tam followed her silently out of the yard. The harbour looked empty and desolate in the pre-dawn light. Winter wind lashed the water. Varjak felt its chill, and shivered.

Holly led them west, following the gang's tracks towards Sally Bones's territory. There were few cars on the road; no people on the pavements. Old snow lay in drifts on the streets. It was hardening into slippery ice. Varjak's pads kept skidding beneath him; he had to fight to keep his balance on the treacherous ground.

In the distance, he could hear an eerie howling.

It was wordless, but it seemed to be telling him something. *Don't come here*, it seemed to say. *Turn back and go away.*

'What's that howling?' he wondered, the fur on the back of his neck prickling.

'It's coming from the Storm Drain,' said Holly, looking at an ugly concrete structure, off the road. 'Don't ever go there. They say wild things live in it – right, Tam?'

'Don't know,' panted Tam. 'Never been there. Never want to!'

They kept away from the Storm Drain, and followed the tracks west. They came to a crossroads on the border of Sally Bones's territory. There was a building site this side of the crossroads. The earth had been overturned; the ground was ripped open. Machines with iron claws stood poised over pits dug deep in the ground. The buildings here were half-demolished, their foundations exposed. A wrecking

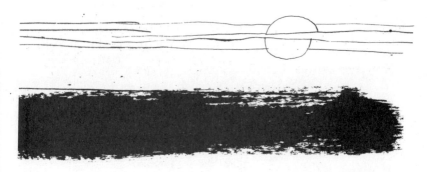

ball dangled from a crane, idle at this time of day.

On the other side of the crossroads, great glass buildings rose from the earth, towering over the city. They pierced the belly of the sky, their upper reaches invisible. They looked sharp-edged and steely in the pre-dawn light.

Varjak's Awareness started to tingle. There was something familiar up ahead. An unnatural scent, ghostly. He edged forwards – and as he reached the crossroads, he saw where it came from.

A tail. A cat's tail. Laid out in the gutter, where people wouldn't see it, but clear as a traffic light to any passing cat. And just along from it – mangled, filthy, but unmistakable – a pair of ears. Soft, furry ears.

Cats' ears.

Varjak stepped back a pace. His mouth had gone dry. Ears and a tail, on their own? What were they doing here in the gutter? It didn't make sense. Varjak's own ears flattened; his tail curled up tight. To lose them – the thought was too horrible.

'Oh – my—' said Holly. She'd just seen them.

Tam shut her eyes. 'I warned you. I warned you, but you wouldn't listen.'

Holly shook her fur, as if shaking out water. 'It's all right,' she said. 'It's nothing to do with us. Let's keep going.'

'I wouldn't do that if I was you,' came a voice from ahead.

Standing in the crossroads, facing them, were two new cats. They were more like lions than cats: powerfully built, with shaggy manes of fur and bushy tails. They moved a little slowly, but they were the biggest, strongest-looking cats Varjak had ever seen. The one who'd spoken was about Razor's height, but he was incredibly stocky and broad across the chest. The other one was even larger.

'I said, I wouldn't do that,' repeated the stocky one. His paws were blunt and dusty. 'Don't you know whose territory this is?'

'Course we do,' said Holly, backing away from the crossroads.

'So what are you doing here?' said the stocky one. 'Can't you see what's in the gutter?'

Varjak glanced at the ears and tail again. His heart sank. Holly didn't seem to know these cats. Were they from Sally Bones's gang? They sounded like it – and their faces were scarred, like Razor's.

'We're just going,' said Holly.

'Oh no you're not!' The two cats strode forwards, rugged manes bristling. Varjak, Holly and Tam backed away, towards a half-demolished building on the site behind them.

'We're looking for an outlaw,' said the stocky one. 'A silver-blue cat called Varjak Paw, who fights like Sally Bones. Is that you?' He squinted slowly at Varjak.

'Him?' laughed Holly at once. 'That's a good one! He's just a pet who got lost – aren't you, Snowflake?'

'Er – that's right!' said Varjak. Sharp as ever, Holly had seen these cats could be bluffed. His only chance was to play along. 'I'm Snowflake, and I'm lost. I'm looking for my home – can you help me?' He smiled sweetly, though his pulse was racing.

The stocky cat scratched his head. 'He's a funny-looking thing, isn't he? I thought Varjak Paw would be bigger – didn't you, Ozzie?'

'Yup,' said the giant cat, speaking at last.

'I don't think he can be the one we're after. But go on, see what he's made of. Might as well.'

Ozzie beamed. 'OK, Omar. Thanks!'

Varjak braced himself as Ozzie squared up to fight. This was a test. If he used the Way, they'd know who he was, and that would be that. He had to face Ozzie without it – and without his friends. Holly and Tam couldn't help him any more, because Omar was keeping them in check.

'There's no need for this!' growled Holly. 'We don't want to fight.'

'No one wants to fight Ozzie!' crowed Omar. 'But you've got no choice!'

Ozzie came barrelling through the air. Varjak rolled aside just in time, but the giant caught his flank as he went: a glancing blow, powerful enough to knock him over.

Varjak came up into a crouch, defending his flank as he got his breath back. How could he beat a cat like this without his Skills? Even with them, he'd struggle against an opponent so immensely big and strong.

Ozzie marched forwards, legs thick like lamp posts. Varjak backed up into the building site. The ground was strewn with rubble. With three steps, he was up against a wall, and Ozzie was still coming. A huge paw shot out. Varjak ducked. Ozzie hit the wall above him. A cloud of dust rose where Varjak's head had been.

He had to get away! A hit like that could kill him! He feinted left, right, but wherever he turned, Ozzie was still in the way. The giant cat grinned, lifted Varjak clean off his paws, and sent him crashing into the wall.

Varjak twisted in mid-air, but couldn't avoid the impact. His bones jarred. His vision blurred. Above, he saw the crane, the wrecking ball, the broken buildings. Ozzie was squaring up to finish him off.

'You'd better run!' whooped Omar. 'It's your only chance!'

Varjak staggered to his paws, heart pounding, out of breath. He wanted to run, desperately – but he knew Ozzie would only catch him. It's useless trying to fight, he thought. I can't beat this cat for power. But if I could somehow use his own power against him . . .

He held himself still, in front of the wall. His heart was thumping like a jackhammer, but he stood his ground, and beckoned to Ozzie. 'Is that all you can do?' he called. 'I thought you were supposed to be strong!'

Ozzie looked startled for a second. Then he pawed the ground – and charged at Varjak with maximum force. Varjak stood there, totally still, till the last possible moment – and then dived under the charge.

CRUNCH!

The giant crashed head-first into the wall. Varjak sprang away, breathing hard. The fight was surely finished. He turned to look – but Ozzie was just dusting himself off!

'*Yee-haa!*' yelled Omar. 'You can't hurt Oz – he can't feel a thing!'

Ozzie grinned a gap-toothed grin. He looked like he was having fun. 'Oh, but he's good, Omar, he's brave! I think he's the one! Can I fight him some more? Please?'

'No, that's enough, little brother,' said Omar, suddenly very serious. He turned to Varjak. 'I only saw one cat who didn't run away from Ozzie before, and that was Sally Bones. So you must be Varjak Paw – and those stories must be true.'

With those words, they bowed down before Varjak. So did Ozzie. They flattened themselves into the rubble before him. 'At your service,' they said together. 'Omar and Ozzie, the Orrible Twins. The strongest cats in town!'

Varjak stared at them in disbelief. Holly and Tam were staring too.

'You're not in Sally Bones's gang, are you?' said Holly. 'You're outlaws! I remember now, Luger said they were looking for twin cats, one big, one bigger.'

'Outlaws, and proud of it,' said Omar, standing up again.

'Outlaws?' breathed Tam. She groomed her bushy tail. 'We're outlaws too!'

'We weren't always,' said Omar. 'We were in Ginger's gang, in the old days, before Sally Bones. Then she made us join *her* gang. It was a nightmare. She used to slash us, just to prove she was Boss. We're stronger than her, but she – she's the only one who knows that secret way of fighting.'

Ozzie flinched. The scar on his face quivered. 'Don't say it, Omar. I don't want to remember. Anyway, we got away from her. And now we've met the cat who's going to put this city right – Snowflake!' He looked at Varjak, and grinned his gap-toothed grin. 'You're not really called Snowflake, are you?'

Varjak couldn't help grinning back. 'No, I'm not,' he said. 'You're right: I'm Varjak.'

'So why were you *really* going to her territory?' said Omar.

'A patrol took a friend of ours away last night,' said Holly. 'A kitten.'

Omar glanced at the ears and tail in the gutter. 'Your friend needs help.'

'What do you know about those ears?' said Varjak.

'You don't know?' said Omar. 'It's—'

'Don't say it,' said Holly. 'It's too horrible.'

'That's why it needs to be said.' Omar clenched his big, blunt paws. '*Because that is Sally Bones's mark.* That's the punishment for breaking her law. She rips your ears and tail off, and leaves them out for everyone to see.'

'What? She can't do that!' Varjak looked at Holly, hoping she'd say Omar was wrong, it was some kind of mistake – but she didn't.

'You remember that – that *animal* we saw outside the secret alleys?' she said. 'That was a cat. A cat with no ears and tail.'

Varjak's mind started to spin. So now he knew why Tam was so scared. And why the street cats in the yard went silent when he'd mentioned it.

'Nobody stops her?' he whispered.

'Nobody can,' said Omar. 'And if you don't act fast, this is what'll happen to your friend.'

Varjak's face burned. This was outrageous. The

most outrageous thing he'd ever heard. He turned away, but everyone was looking at him. He could feel it; and he could feel his own power, rising inside him like a flame.

'No,' he said, striding into the crossroads. 'It's not going to happen to Jess.'

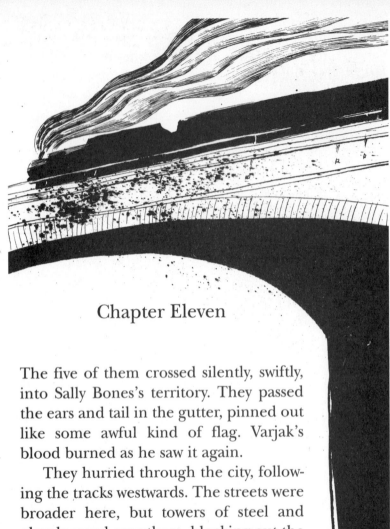

Chapter Eleven

The five of them crossed silently, swiftly, into Sally Bones's territory. They passed the ears and tail in the gutter, pinned out like some awful kind of flag. Varjak's blood burned as he saw it again.

They hurried through the city, following the tracks westwards. The streets were broader here, but towers of steel and glass loomed over them, blocking out the sky with walls no cat could climb. They were so much taller than the brown

buildings of the harbour. Varjak felt like he was running through a canyon. The sun was just beginning to rise, shooting streaks of crimson onto the glass. Dawn was fast approaching.

The trail led down to the riverside. As the river came into view, Varjak heard water rushing past, but it was drowned out by a shrill whistle and a rattling roar. These noises came from a railway bridge that spanned the river. A train was hurtling over, making the bridge shake and shake and shake. It made Varjak's fur shake too, and put his teeth on edge.

This part of town was so different to the harbour. It looked like the riverbanks had been eaten up by towers. Chimney stacks belched out smoke. The taste of burning was thick on the air. Across the river, Varjak could see one tower that stood out from the rest, set apart on a mound. It was stone, not glass, and it looked very old. It might've been white once, but now it was black with smoke stains. It looked like a jagged claw of darkness, tearing into the dawn.

'That's Sally Bones's place,' whispered Omar. 'The graveyard. She only comes out of it at night. If you end up there, it's over. But down here by the river: this is where they bring prisoners first, to soften them up.'

He led them to the top of a rickety wooden gang-plank that led down to the waterfront. It juddered as a train went by. The railway bridge stretched far off into the night, across a wide expanse of water. Most of the river was calm and still. Just under the bridge, though, it churned with dirty brown froth.

That's strange, thought Varjak. Why's it churning like that?

He crept to the edge of the gangplank. It was low tide, so the river's muddy banks were exposed. There was no sign of Sally Bones – but there were six of her gang just below him. Six brawny tomcats. One of them was pinning Jess flat in the mud. Three others were watching from a distance, laughing. Razor was looking out at the river, alone. Luger was leaning over Jess and shouting: 'WHERE IS HE? WHERE IS HE? TELL US!'

Jess didn't answer. Luger nodded at the tomcat pinning her down. The tomcat grinned, placed a claw over her ear – and ripped right through it.

Jess screamed.

On the gangplank, Varjak rose up, and sprang towards Jess. 'That's enough!' he growled. Fury darkened his sight. He breathed deep, filling his lungs with grim purpose – *in–two–three–four, out–two––three–four.*

The world seemed to shimmer and slow down around him. The power rose up inside him. And now he made a Moving Circle –

'Stop!' called Holly. 'We need to plan!'

– but Varjak couldn't stop. He was too angry. The power seethed inside him. As he touched down on the riverbank, it built up, and up, and up, until it was more than he could contain or control – and then it flung him forwards towards Jess.

His body arced through the air, a Moving Circle of pure energy, pulsing, glowing, throbbing with rage. Luger jerked away, just in time. Varjak turned to the tomcat who was pinning Jess down: and the power exploded.

SMASH! SMASH! SMASH!

The tomcat crumpled. He sank into the ground. Something splattered on Varjak's fur. Mud, perhaps, or blood. The tomcat was very still. Up on the railway bridge, a train whistle shrieked into the dawn.

Varjak roared, full of ferocious joy. There were five more cats to fight. But the power was so strong. It felt so good. He wasn't scared of it any more. It was flowing all around him, like a ring of fire, and at the back of his throat was the taste of burning.

'Jess!' he yelled. 'Get up!'

Her ear was torn and bleeding, but her eyes opened wide at his voice. 'Varjak? Am I dreaming?'

'You're coming home.'

Razor edged forwards. 'Wait!' he said. 'I have to talk to you.'

There was a strange expression in his eyes that Varjak couldn't read. But there was no time to wonder what it meant. His Awareness screamed with danger. Behind him, another tomcat was coming to get him.

Varjak spun round. Arced under the blow. And

came up into the cat's belly. He felt the crunch of ribs, and then the tomcat was spinning through the air. He splashed into the river, and was carried away by the tide. The train was gone now; its juddering roar had faded. Under the railway bridge, the river still bubbled and seethed, a torrent of dirty brown water.

Two down – but now Varjak was off-balance, and Luger was coming at him. Varjak tried to turn.

Too late.

Luger smashed into him, breaking the Circle. Varjak reeled back in the mud, exposed. And now Luger was coming in for the kill –

– but Holly got there first! She sprang down from the gangplank, and wrestled Luger away. He was much bigger than her, and stronger, but Holly had the advantage of surprise; and now Omar and Tam were with her, backing her up, and Ozzie was charging into the other two Bones cats.

'Omar! Ozzie!' Luger shouted. 'You traitors – the Boss wants you, dead or alive!'

'She'll never get us,' growled Omar. He thumped Luger hard, sending him sprawling into the mud. 'We're in Varjak's gang now!'

Jess's eyes glowed. 'Who are *they*?' she whispered.

'The Orrible Twins!' said Varjak. 'Outlaw cats. They're with us.'

Ozzie was on the rampage. The two Bones cats

fled from him down the waterfront. Omar and Holly were holding Luger face down in the mud. Only Razor was still standing now, and he was completely out-numbered.

'Let's get out of here!' shouted Holly. She moved back towards the gangplank; Omar and Ozzie followed her. Varjak started another Moving Circle, and helped Jess to her paws.

'Can you still run?' he said.

'Try and stop me!'

They joined the others at the bottom of the gangplank. Razor stood where he was, looking at Varjak. High above, there was an ear-splitting whistle, and the railway bridge started to rattle again, to rattle and roar with the rush of another train.

'You won't get away with this!' shouted Luger, hauling himself up from the mud.

'Leave us alone,' said Varjak. 'We're free cats, and nobody hurts a free cat.' His Circle shimmered like silver-blue fire in the night.

'Wait!' said Razor, still looking at Varjak. 'I want to—'

His words were drowned out by the roar of the train. Varjak and his friends started to climb the gangplank, Ozzie holding the line at the rear. Luger lashed out as they went. Ozzie took the blow without flinching, and hit back with his huge paws. Luger fell away. Razor just stood at the foot of the gangplank, watching in the mud, as they made it to the top.

'Go!' panted Holly. 'Go, go, go!'

They raced away into a red dawn. Jess was still bleeding, but she ran the fastest, and no one was left behind.

As the streets flashed by, as they dashed through the great glass canyons, Varjak came out of Slow-Time. It was hard. His throat felt raw. His vision was blurry.

But somehow, through the chaos and confusion, they made it back to the border of the West side. No one followed them; they met no patrols. They scrambled over the crossroads, past the ears and tail in the gutter, and back into the city centre.

They'd done it. They'd gone into Sally Bones's territory, and brought Jess out alive.

And up above, the snow began to fall again, to fall unstoppably from the sky.

Chapter Twelve

Back in the harbour, the morning sun shone down on the river. Ships' horns rang out as they came in to dock. Flags fluttered on their masts.

Varjak and his friends walked down into the snowy yard. It felt like coming home. There were the brown buildings again, their windows lit with a cosy glow. There were the street cats, most of them still sleeping. Mrs Moggs sat by the ship's anchor, Old Buckley by her side. As soon as they saw Jess coming, they ran out to greet her.

'My Jessie?' cried Mrs Moggs. 'They brought my Jessie back!'

Her cry woke the yard. In moments, the street cats were up and buzzing, eyes aglow.

'They did it!' The word went round like wildfire.

'Varjak's brought our Jessie back!'

Up above, seagulls rose high on the river breeze.

'What happened, my dears?' said Mrs Moggs, licking Jess, comforting her.

'They was about to rip my ears and tail off!' breathed Jess. 'I thought I was finished, but then Varjak rescued me—'

Old Buckley shook his head. 'How? How could he do that?'

'He fights like nothing you ever seen, Buckley. *Bam! Bam! Bam!* He's even better than Sally Bones!'

'Then I owe you an apology, Mr Varjak Paw,' said Old Buckley. 'I was wrong about you!' His face broke out into the gladdest grin.

Varjak felt so proud of that grin. 'Well, it wasn't just me,' he said. 'It was all of us.'

'Varjak's got a gang now,' said Jess. 'Them two big cats, they're outlaws, but they're with us!'

'Pleased to meet you,' said the Orrible Twins.

Around them, snow was shimmering down from the sky, coating the yard in white. Varjak looked at

Omar and Ozzie, at Holly and Tam, at Jess – and his skin tingled beneath his fur. We've done it, he thought. We've done the impossible.

'We're lucky we got there in time,' said Holly. 'If Sally Bones had been there—'

'You was clever, going at dawn,' said Mrs Moggs. 'Course, she'll come back at us. You can depend on it. But we don't care, do we?'

A defiant cheer rang round the yard.

'Varjak told 'em,' said Jess fiercely. 'He told 'em we're the Free Cats, and no one hurts a Free Cat.'

'The Free Cats, eh?' said Old Buckley. 'It's a good name. We never had a name before.'

'It's time that changed,' said Mrs Moggs. 'From now on, no one can march in here and take us away, or steal our food. This'll be a free city – for Free Cats!'

The Free Cats whooped. They started dancing in the snow, like these were words they'd never dared to say aloud, but words they'd held secretly in their hearts for the longest time. And the way they were looking at Varjak – especially Mrs Moggs and Jess – his heart was dancing too, for it filled him with a rush of pride that swirled inside him like snowflakes in the dark.

'Tonight, let's forget them and their laws,' cried Mrs Moggs. 'Let's eat like proper cats again!'

And they did. Through the day, as Varjak and his

friends rested, the Free Cats went out into the harbour. Defying Sally Bones's law, they returned with heaps of food, more than they could eat. They found no patrols out there; no sign of Sally Bones's gang.

'They're scared of Varjak!' some cats said.

'They're biding their time,' said others.

No one knew for sure. But as evening fell, there was a feast in the harbour yard, greater than anyone could remember. The street cats sank their teeth into fresh fish from the river, the food they'd been denied for so long. There was a wild thrill in the air. The brown buildings were decked out with strings of coloured lights, strung between the windows. The snow was shimmering down, light and powder white, and up above the yard, all the stars were coming out.

'This is delicious!' said Holly, relishing the feast.

'Best food we've had all winter,' said Omar. 'Right, little brother?'

'Mmm,' said Ozzie, tucking into another juicy fish.

'Why do you call him little brother?' said Jess. 'He's bigger than you.'

'He's younger,' said Omar. 'I'm the older Twin. I have to look after him – don't I, Oz?'

Ozzie smiled shyly, showing his gap-toothed grin. 'Yup, I'd be lost without Omar telling me what to do all the time!' Everyone laughed.

'This is great,' said Tam, licking her lips. 'If only we had some mice for dessert—'

'We haven't seen a mouse all winter,' said Omar. 'You've got to be a fearless hunter to find one of them.'

Tam grinned. 'Oh, I saw one a few days ago – didn't I, Varjak? Fearless Tam the Hunter, that's me!' Varjak smiled, and Holly rolled her eyes, but Omar looked impressed.

'Would you come hunting with me, Fearless Tam?' he said.

'Hunting – with you?' Her chocolate-brown eyes widened with alarm. 'But – I'm not really fearless – I was just—'

'Don't worry,' said Omar. 'I'm useless! Everyone's good at different things, right? Me, I can fight the best of them – but I never did get the hang of hunting.'

Tam giggled. 'Bet you I'm worse! Come on, then. Let's look for some dessert!' They headed together out of the yard, Tam's bushy tail swinging proudly behind her. Ozzie started to follow them.

'No, you wait here, little brother,' said Omar over his shoulder, eyes flashing. 'I'll bring you something back.' Ozzie blinked, and stood there looking lost as his brother left the yard with Tam.

'What you standing there for?' said Jess, grabbing the giant. 'There's food to eat, for once!' She dragged Ozzie off to feast with the Free Cats, leaving

Varjak alone with Holly, by the back wall. Above their heads, fire escapes zigzagged up to the rooftops, and the open sky beyond.

'Omar and Ozzie are funny, aren't they?' said Varjak. 'I'm glad they're on our side. We wouldn't have made it without them.'

'It's not over yet,' said Holly. 'It's great that the Free Cats are so happy – but what's going to happen when Sally Bones finds out? I don't believe she's scared. Do you?'

Varjak glanced over at the Free Cats, celebrating in the snow. All they needed was someone to stand up for them. And I can do that, he told himself. I can fight. My power's getting stronger all the time. Remember what Jess said? *He's even better than Sally Bones!*

He flexed his paws with determination. 'We'll deal with that if we have to,' he said. 'The main thing is, we saved Jess. And if we could do that – well, maybe we can do anything.'

Holly gazed up at the sky. So did Varjak. Once again, he thought how magical the city seemed in the snow and starlight. At that moment, Holly didn't look like the spiky cat he knew; a cat who'd seen too much of the world, and had grown all gravelly to protect herself. She looked like the kitten she must have been, full of mischief and tales and wild, wild dreams.

'Do you really think so?' she whispered, like she was daring herself to believe it.

Something lit up in Varjak then, something bright and warm that shone through the winter night. It felt like a string of lights, strung between two windows, linking them together. It felt like whiskers of starlight, fine and strong between them.

'I think we can do anything we like,' he said, 'you and me.'

She smiled. 'Well, there's no going back from here. You've started something big, and I'm with you all the way, whatever happens.' She paused, and looked down. 'But who knows what's going to happen? We might not be together so much . . .'

Varjak felt those whiskers of starlight, touching somewhere so deep inside, it made him dizzy.

'I wouldn't—' he started, and stopped, and tried again. 'Holly, I don't think any of this would make sense without you,' he said.

She nodded quietly. They spoke no more; there was no need.

After a moment, she curled up beside him, placed a paw on top of his own, and closed her eyes as their tails twined together. Her breathing grew slow and steady. Her face looked so calm, so peaceful. He could feel her fur, touching his; black-and-white mixing into silver-blue. Slowly, his eyes closed, and his breathing dropped to match her own.

They lay there like that, close and comfortable, the starlight strong between them, until they fell asleep.

Chapter Thirteen

Varjak dreamed.

It was sunrise in Mesopotamia. He breathed in the wild mint air. Everything seemed brighter and clearer than normal; the sky so clear and blue, he saw stars shining through the sunlight.

He was climbing the mountain with Jalal. They were on a path, rising higher and higher. He couldn't see the summit from here. There was still a long way to go.

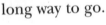

The path narrowed, and Varjak found himself at the foot of a high, overhanging cliff. Through the middle of the cliff, there was a crack just wide enough for a cat, but it was blocked by a stone.

'I'll just move this stone, Jalal,' he said, 'and then we can go on.'

'Indeed?' said Jalal. 'And can you see the stone you propose to move?'

'Of course! It's right in front of me.'

'If you can see that stone,' said Jalal, in a slow, patient tone, 'then you can see everything it is, every-thing it was, everything it will be.'

Varjak frowned. The stone was in their way, and all Jalal could do was talk in riddles, in that irritating tone of voice.

'Yes, I know how to see, Jalal,' he said. He reached out a paw, and pushed the stone. It didn't budge, so he tried pulling instead.

This time, the stone came away, and rolled down the mountain behind him.

There was a soft shifting sound. A pebble rolled out of the gap Varjak had made. That stone must've been the one thing holding it back. He stood aside and watched as it rolled on down the mountain.

More pebbles came out of the gap. Then stones started to come, and bigger stones. It seemed like the gap was getting wider, and the stones kept coming, speeding up as they came. More and more stone was rolling out now, and snow was coming with it. The shifting noise was changing, too. It was turning into a rumble, a deep, earthy rumble – and then a cracking, crunching noise came out of the cliff-face.

'Stand aside!' shouted Jalal. They moved away just in time, for with a great sighing, groaning sound, the whole cliff came tumbling down.

The air was full of dust and snow and debris. Where the cliff had been, there was now a torrent of rock and snow, rolling fast and hard. Varjak looked up, and saw the side of the mountain above him shifting, saw massive drifts of snow shake and slide. He felt the earth beneath his paws shudder, and his heart was in his mouth, because he'd never dreamed of anything like this before.

'What's happening, Jalal?' he cried.

'You have started an avalanche,' said Jalal, very calmly.

Varjak watched, open-mouthed, as the torrent of snow grew, gathered, rock and snow, growing bigger, getting faster; and further down the mountainside, he could see flocks of birds flapping, animals running for cover, the world turning head over heels as the mighty mountain crumbled. Sheets of ice came sliding down, blocks as big as buildings, scything through the snow; and Varjak thought of that first stone, that one little stone he'd pulled away, and he shook his head in fear and wonder.

Slowly, the avalanche settled. The rolling and rumbling came to rest; the rock and snow found new formations. The shaking stopped, and beneath the clear blue starry sky, the mountain grew calm and still once more.

'Now, if you had truly seen that stone,' said Jalal, 'then you would have seen all this, too. No action, however small, is without consequence. But come now. For better or worse, you have opened a way forward.'

Chapter Fourteen

Varjak opened his eyes. The dream was over. It was night and he was in the harbour yard. Holly was pulling away from him. The warmth of her body faded as the winter wind whipped between them.

'Holly, what's wrong?' he said.

She opened her mouth to speak, but no words came out. Her fur was standing on end. She was staring at something over his shoulder. He'd never seen her look so scared.

He turned round.

And wished that he hadn't.

A thin white cat sat behind him. She was watching him with one ice-blue eye. Where the other eye should've been, there was nothing but shadow. Her white fur was spotless clean, but around her was the smell of darkness, of dank and deadly things and places.

It was Sally Bones.

'Varjak Paw,' she hissed. 'The cat who thinks he can fight.'

Varjak flinched at her words, as though his body knew something he'd tried to forget. Her teeth tapered down to deadly points. Her ribs jutted out of her side, like they were trying to escape from her. She was so thin and white, he could scarcely see her against the snow. Only Sally Bones's eye, like a chip of bluest ice, glittering in the night.

Slowly, out of the darkness, appeared her gang around her: Luger, Razor, and the rest. They were all tough cats, big and brawny, their fur short and bristly – yet they looked like soft little kittens compared to her.

Varjak's friends crept up beside him, under the fire escapes: Holly, Tam and Jess, Omar and Ozzie. The Twins looked paralysed with fear. At a single glance from Sally Bones, their proud manes seemed to shrivel.

The Free Cats weren't feasting any more. They were staring at Sally Bones. They were watching and waiting, to see what she would do.

Varjak cursed to himself. So stupid. How could he let her find him sleeping? She'd caught him with his guard down. But it wasn't too late.

He breathed in–two–three–four. The power rose up in him, hot and strong. He was in Slow-Time now. He was facing her: the other cat who knew the Way.

Sally Bones shook her head. She breathed in, and her body started to shimmer with a terrible power. She was in Slow-Time too. But she was faster than Varjak. She was faster than anything. She reached out a paw, and brushed the tips of his whiskers lightly, almost gently, with a claw.

That was all it took.

Varjak came crashing out of Slow-Time. He couldn't stop himself. It was like falling from the sky,

smack into solid earth. The power faded. The energy ebbed away. He couldn't even meet her eye, for her power was so much greater than his own. He'd felt it the last time they'd met – and now, from the tips of his whiskers to the end of his tail, he knew it once again.

He was beaten, without even a fight.

His friends' heads dropped. The Free Cats looked away.

'Varjak Paw,' said Sally Bones. 'You have broken

the law. You have hunted. You have trespassed on my territory. And now you have shed blood. We will not tolerate this. We will defend ourselves. You will pay for what you have done.'

She paused, to let the words sink in. Varjak couldn't speak. There was ice in his belly. Ice in his brain. His face felt frozen where she'd touched him.

Mrs Moggs stood up. She left the anchor and chain where she'd been sitting, and walked up to Varjak and Sally Bones. Old Buckley shuffled behind her, shivering through the snow.

'Well now,' said Mrs Moggs. 'I think there must be some mistake. Varjak's a good cat. He'd never shed blood, not without reason.'

The ice in Varjak's belly cracked with shame. Mrs Moggs was standing up for him – but wasn't he meant to be standing up for the Free Cats? Now, when it really mattered, he couldn't do it. He couldn't even defend himself, let alone his friends.

'Why are you taking this outlaw's side?' said Sally Bones.

'Your thugs took my Jessie,' said Mrs Moggs. Her voice was quiet but firm. 'That Razor, and Luger, and them others – they took her, when she done nothing wrong. All Varjak did was bring her back. And if some of your gang got hurt, that's their own fault.'

Sally Bones gazed round the yard, at the remains of the feast. 'I see you have been eating fish. Have you forgotten the law? That food is for us. It is not for you.'

'That law's not fair,' said Mrs Moggs. 'That law's no law at all.'

Behind her, Old Buckley squirmed. 'She – she don't mean it!' he stuttered. 'Please don't hurt her!'

Sally Bones ignored him. 'If you break the law,' she told Mrs Moggs, 'you get punished. What could be fairer than that?' She came right up to Mrs Moggs, and stared at the marmalade tabby with her ice-blue eye. Mrs Moggs stared right back. The moment stretched out, and still Sally Bones kept looking and looking, deeper and deeper into Mrs Moggs's eyes. Then at last she spoke.

'I see what happened,' said the thin white cat. 'You got so carried away when Varjak brought your Jessie back, that you started getting ideas about feasting, and being free. Yes?'

A smile flickered across Mrs Moggs's face. 'Yes,' she said. 'And I'm proud of it.'

'Then you will face justice too.' Sally Bones turned to her gang, and snapped out her orders. 'Luger. Razor. Find every single law-breaker in this place, and prepare them for punishment.'

Varjak shuddered. Sally Bones's punishment: the ears and tails.

'Something wrong, Razor?' said Sally Bones. The tiger-striped tomcat hadn't moved; he was standing in the snow, looking at Varjak with the same strange expression in his eyes as before.

'Nothing, Boss,' he said. 'I just—'

'He's lost his nerve!' spat Luger. 'He didn't even try to stop Varjak Paw escaping, by the river. He just watched us get beaten.'

Sally Bones stalked up to Razor. Her white tail swished behind her like a whip.

Razor's body pressed low into the snow. 'No, Boss – I – I can explain—' he stammered.

Sally Bones stared into his eyes, silent. After an endless moment, she shook her head. 'You are no longer in my gang,' she said.

The air shimmered. There was a blur of white so fast, Varjak barely even saw it.

Razor howled. There was a fresh slash mark on his face, bright red and raw. And Sally Bones was flicking the blood from her long white claws.

Razor bolted, howling with pain. He fled up the stairs, into the night.

'Finish him at your leisure,' Sally Bones told Luger. 'But first: round up the law-breakers.'

'Yes, Boss. It'll be a pleasure.'

'No!' cried Mrs Moggs. 'You got no right! Leave us alone!'

But already, Sally Bones's gang were moving among the Free Cats, pushing, shoving, herding them together.

Varjak just watched. For all his Skills, he felt powerless before the thin white cat. He looked at his friends. They were all powerless. Around the harbour yard, lights were going out in windows. The brown buildings were falling into darkness.

Sally Bones leaned in close to Varjak, under the fire escapes, as her gang went about their work. She spoke in his ear, so no one else could hear. Her breath was like frost.

'Now tell me where you learned the Way,' she hissed. 'Not another cat alive knows what you know.'

Varjak quivered. His whole body was shaking. 'I – I learned it in Mesopotamia,' he mumbled.

'There is no Mesopotamia!' said Sally Bones bitterly. 'Tell me the truth!'

She looked deep into his eyes, like she'd looked at Mrs Moggs, and Razor. Varjak wanted to turn away, but he couldn't. He couldn't move. Her ice-blue eye was burning into his brain. It felt like she was looking right inside him, probing his thoughts, seeing his secrets. She was opening him up, stripping him bare, layer by layer.

He tried to resist, but she was so strong. She had him in her grip, and she was going deeper and deeper, into his core.

Varjak felt faint. Ice in his belly; ice in his brain. Black spots danced before his eyes, filled his vision. It was as if Sally Bones was draining everything good

119

and bright out of him. He could see nothing before him now but darkness.

Cold fear clawed at his heart. Darkness and despair scratched his eyes. The desire to give up. Give up and die.

'Yes,' murmured Sally Bones. 'Give in to the darkness. *Give up your dreams.*'

And in Varjak's mind, just for a moment, there was the sharp sweet scent of mint, and a bright and silent sunrise –

– and Sally Bones gasped.

'No!' she cried. 'No!' She pulled away from him, and staggered back in the snow. Her ice-blue eye was shut.

Suddenly, Varjak was free. Her grip on him was gone. He could move again.

Mrs Moggs had seen it all. 'Quick!' she yelled. 'Run! Up that fire escape – and take my Jessie with you!'

Varjak ran. Bolted like he'd been burned. His friends followed right behind him. Tam, Omar, Ozzie, Jess, Holly: they all scrambled up the fire escape. But even as they raced towards the rooftops, Sally Bones's voice echoed after them.

'Stop them!' she screamed. 'Bring the outlaws back here!'

Chapter Fifteen

Varjak climbed for his life. The steps were slippery with ice. His paws skidded as he scrambled up.

'Faster!' panted Holly behind him. 'They're coming!'

Sally Bones's gang were stalking towards the fire escape. They looked unstoppable. Only Mrs Moggs stood before them, blocking their way. A few Free Cats rallied round her. Her marmalade fur looked bright and brave against the ice-white snow.

Varjak's heart was exploding in his chest. He didn't want to leave her behind, yet she'd told him to go.

The power was very far from him now. His brain felt bruised. How could Sally Bones enter his thoughts like that? Why did she pull away? He didn't understand – but there was no time for questions. He had to get away!

'What's happening?' said Jess, above him.

'Keep climbing,' said Holly. 'Don't look.'

They kept going up the steps. A gust of wind swirled a snow flurry before them, blocking their view. They climbed into darkness. Varjak thought he heard a scream from below, but couldn't be sure.

When he looked down again, the little cluster of Free Cats was surrounded. Sally Bones's gang swarmed round them like angry black dots on the snow. They were so much bigger and stronger than the Free Cats. But they couldn't climb the steps, because in the middle of it all, Mrs Moggs wouldn't yield to them. How long could she hold out? Varjak looked away. He kept climbing. Up. Just keep going up.

'Varjak!' shouted Jess, a moment later. 'Varjak, look!'

He didn't want to. But he steadied himself against the wind, and looked down. A circle of space had opened around the fire escape. At its centre, he saw Sally Bones, shimmering with a terrible power. Beside her in the circle of space was Mrs Moggs.

But Mrs Moggs wasn't moving. And all about her, the snow was staining red.

'No!' screamed Jess. 'NO! NO! NO!'

The wind was howling like a wild animal. The fire escape was shaking like it would break in two. Varjak had to hold Jess back, because she was mad with grief and rage; or maybe he was holding himself back, because Mrs Moggs was in terrible trouble.

But so was he. Sally Bones's gang began to swarm

up the fire escape. Mrs Moggs had held them off for a few precious moments, but no one stood in their way any more.

'The rooftops!' yelled Holly. 'We have to make it to the top!'

They hauled themselves up. The steps grew narrower and shakier the higher they went. Varjak glanced back as he reached the top. Sally Bones's gang were climbing fast, closing in.

He scrabbled onto the roof.

It was so high up here. Exposed and precarious. The wind came in wild, sudden gusts. It was a flat roof with an open drop: no railings, nothing to hold onto. There was a huge chasm between it and the next roof, spanned only by electrical cables.

The city was spread out below. On one side was a glowing network of amber lights, criss-crossing the city centre. On the other side was the river, cutting through the lights like a huge black snake, coiling through the night. Far beyond it, in the distance, stood those great glass towers: Sally Bones's territory.

Varjak felt dizzy. The wind roared in his ears. The night sky was like a blanket over the city, a starless blanket of darkness that covered everything and everyone, darkness without end.

Rooftops lay ahead of him, to the left, and to the right – but they were all so far away. Much further than he could jump.

'What now?' said Omar.

Holly scouted the edge of the roof. 'Have a look at this,' she said.

They joined her at the edge. A thin red electrical line dangled between the rooftops, swaying in the wind.

Tam drew back from it, eyes closed. 'Oh, no,' she said. 'No way. I'm not crossing *that*.'

'It's this or Sally Bones,' urged Holly. 'Come on: who's first?'

No one said a word. Varjak looked at Jess. She was shaking.

'Can you do this?' he asked her. She didn't answer. She just looked up at him, eyes wet with helpless rage. 'Will you do it if I go first?' he said. She wiped her eyes, and nodded. 'All right, then,' he said. 'I will.'

He took a deep breath, and strode up to the ledge. He glanced at the thin red line. He tried to picture it in his mind as a line painted on a road,

safely down on the street; not a perilous
thread, strung high above the city.

It didn't help. But Holly was right. It
was this or Sally Bones. And anything –
anything – was better than Sally Bones.

Varjak placed a paw on the cable. It
wobbled under his weight – but it held.
Now he put another paw down, and
another, and now all four paws were off
the rooftop, and he was balanced finely
in space, tail held out behind him. He
could feel the wind, gusting through his
fur, making him sway left and right. The
cable wobbled.

He didn't look up or down: just
straight ahead. This is what you have to
do, he told himself. Just go, and keep
going till you reach the other side.

He inched forwards across the void,
inch by inch, paw by paw. The cable

swayed and rocked with every step. Snow whipped into his face. His stomach churned. Surely he was going to fall. He was going to die horribly, he was going to –

Keep going. Just keep going. It's all you can do.

He kept going. Paw after paw, he kept going, kept going, kept going – and then, somehow, he didn't know how, a paw touched down on solid ground.

He'd made it to the other side.

'YES!' shouted Holly from the other side. 'Now you, Jess! Next! Next! Next!'

They came one by one: a line of cats crossing this chasm between the buildings. Jess did it with her eyes closed. Tam next. Then Omar, right behind her. As Ozzie crossed, the cable bucked beneath his bulk – but he made it too; until it was just Holly left on the other side.

'Come on, Holly!' called Varjak, feeling light-headed. 'Come on, it's easy—'

And then his heart lurched, and his head swam, and the words froze in his mouth. Because right behind Holly, one of Sally Bones's cats was climbing onto the rooftop.

'Holly!' he yelled. 'Behind you!'

Holly turned, and saw. First one. Then two. Then three of the Bones gang stood on the rooftop with her.

Holly sprang onto the cable. She moved rapidly,

her spiky black-and-white fur rippling in the wind. She made it easily to the middle – but then she stopped and turned to face the Bones cats, poised above that void in space, snow swirling all around her.

'Quick, Holly!' urged Tam. 'You can make it!'

Holly shook her head. Her mustard eyes glinted, unafraid, as she stared at the gang cats. She looked calm and cool, deadly determined. She knew what she was doing – and with a sickening jolt, Varjak saw it too.

'Holly!' he shouted. 'No! You can't—'

But the first of the Bones gang was already on the cable with her. He was a huge, hulking tomcat. Under their combined weight, the thin red line looked taut, tight, ready to snap. Every nerve in Varjak's body screamed at him to get back onto that cable and help her – but it was almost at breaking point. It couldn't take any more pressure.

The Bones cat was nearly on top of Holly. She stood there, facing him, crouching low as he came.

'Go, Varjak!' she called – and as the Bones cat sprang at her, she took the cable in her mouth, sank her teeth in, and cut it clean down the middle.

As Varjak watched in horror, it broke in two halves. Each half unravelled with a shower of sparks and swung back into the buildings on either side. The cable was gone. No one could cross now. Holly had destroyed it.

She twisted about and sprang towards safety, and Varjak's heart shivered with hope. But the Bones cat was quicker. His rough paws seized her back legs, held her, dragged her down into that horrendous gap between the buildings. They fell together, Holly and the Bones cat, whirling like snow and fighting as they fell, and fell, and fell away from view.

Varjak's heart ripped in half. No. No. This can't be happening. Not to Holly, not Holly, anyone but –

'Holly!' he yelled. He clawed at the edge of the roof, shouting her name through the wind and snow.

'HOLLY!' he screamed. He couldn't see her any more. She'd fallen into the void. She was gone.

'Varjak,' said Tam, behind him. 'We have to get out of here.' He hardly heard her. All he knew was that Holly was gone. He'd lost Holly, who he cared about more than anyone in the world; and without her, nothing made sense any more.

'Come on,' said Tam, dragging him back from the edge, through the blizzard of snow. 'She – she knew what she was doing.' He couldn't answer. He had no strength left, no words. Just Holly's name, echoing in his head, over and over and over again.

Varjak let Tam lead him away from the edge, from the void, to safety. Each step away from Holly was like a claw in his heart. He couldn't feel his paws any more; the pads were numb, as if they'd been ripped off or frozen by the ice. And was it just the wind and snow that stung his eyes, so he couldn't see his way clear?

On the other roof, the Bones cats were climbing back down the fire escape. It was only a matter of time before they found another way up.

Varjak's friends moved on first. They made him run in spite of himself. They rushed like the wind across the city skyline. They sprang across gaps where they could. They climbed up and down fire escapes; they went over and under rooftops. They did what it took to get away.

Sometimes they glimpsed Sally Bones's gang in the distance, hunting them, tracking them down. But Holly had broken the trail. She'd made sure they would not be caught. Beneath them, amber street lamps glowed in curving rows, spelling out the shapes of highways and houses, alleys and roads. They followed the lights back home.

The flight over the rooftops took till dawn. They reached the secret alleys as morning lifted the black blanket of the sky, and the first street lamps flickered off. Exhausted, drained, at the end of their strength, they clambered down the fire escapes to their one safe place at last. Cludge welcomed them in with a worried-sounding bark.

They were outlaws, on the run. Sally Bones was after them. They'd lost Holly, and who knew what had become of Mrs Moggs and the Free Cats?

But they hadn't been caught yet. Safe, for the moment, they slumped onto the cobbles, and crashed into sleep.

Chapter Sixteen

Varjak dreamed. He dreamed of the wild mint air and the bright, silent sunlight. He dreamed of a sky so clear and blue, he could see the stars, though it was daytime. He dreamed he was in Mesopotamia with Jalal.

But even in his dreams, his heart was breaking.

'She's gone, Jalal,' he said. 'I've lost her.'

His ancestor made no sign of hearing. He just kept walking, up and up the slope. Varjak walked with him, lost in his own thoughts. That mountain range hung there, huge and perfect as the sky.

After a while, the ground levelled out, and they reached a plateau. Far above was a mountain peak. It towered over them like some jagged claw of rock. Varjak couldn't see a way up. The rock face was sheer; impossible to climb.

He turned. Rising from the plateau behind him was a series of steps carved into the mountainside. The steps led up to an open doorway, an entrance into the mountain itself. A trickle of water flowed out of it, into the silver stream below.

Around this doorway were strange carvings. Images of people and cats; men with the heads of animals, and creatures with the faces of men. It looked like some kind of temple, but it was hard to see clearly, for it was obviously very ancient. The stone was crumbling, and mint grew wild all around. The scent was intoxicating. It filled Varjak's mind.

Jalal padded up the steps. Varjak followed. The steps were littered with debris: pieces of blue and amber stone that had come away from the carvings. Fragments that had once been part of a picture, but now just lay in ruins.

Jalal walked through the entrance into a chamber so dark, Varjak couldn't see the walls; only the glow of his ancestor's eyes, leading him on silently. He followed.

They walked through chambers and down corridors where the only sound was the trickle of water. At last, they came to a place so dark, Varjak couldn't even see Jalal's eyes any more. It was pitch black.

Varjak closed his eyes, and it made no difference to the view.

'Here we are,' came Jalal's voice. 'Here you

may see truly.'

'Here?' said Varjak. 'But I can't see a thing!'

'Keep looking,' said Jalal.

Varjak kept looking. The view didn't change; absolute dark was absolute dark. Yet he felt moisture beneath his paws, and thought he could hear a soft tinkling sound, like a musical note, just below the surface of the silence.

'Can you see it yet?' said Jalal.

'No. But what's that sound?'

'Keep looking.'

Varjak shuffled in the dust. What was the point of this? He was never going to see in here. And the dark was making him nervous, pressing in on him –

'Can you see it now?' said Jalal.

'Of course I can't!' said Varjak. 'You know I can't, and you can't either! This is a place with no light! It's always going to be a place with no light! I'm never going to see anything in here!'

'It is a place with no light,' said Jalal, '*at this moment*. But what seems true at one moment may not be true the next.'

And as he spoke, Varjak blinked, for he thought he saw something. A narrow window in the wall had begun to glow. It was no wider than a whisker, but yes, it was glowing, growing brighter now. Light was coming into the darkness, filling it.

They were standing in a magnificent chamber, full of carvings. Varjak looked up. He saw the ceiling far above him; saw the walls around him; saw Jalal, right beside him. Jalal was gazing down at a pool of water, as blue as the Mesopotamian sky. That was where the tinkling sound came from.

'Just because you cannot see something,' said Jalal, 'does not mean it is not there.'

'But – how?'

'Those mountains are so high, the sun usually passes behind them. Once a year only, for the briefest time, sunrise clears the mountains, and then a single ray of light comes streaming in through that window. At this time – and this time only – light falls upon this pool of water. It is the source of the river. It is completely pure and clear – so clear that we may even see through space and time here, to the truth.'

And now it seemed to Varjak that the water in the pool was flickering, its surface blurring and growing thin. The tinkling sound was changing. It felt like it was calling out to him. He looked closer.

'In there, you will see truly,' said Jalal, 'though the truth may not be what you wish to see. Do you dare?'

Chapter Seventeen

Varjak woke. Mesopotamia was gone. He was back in the secret alleys. It was late afternoon, and a cold wind was blowing through his fur. It was shaking the fire escapes and drainpipes. Somewhere in the distance, a door was banging open and shut, open and shut in the wind.

He could see Omar and Ozzie, Tam and Jess, huddled by those grilles in the ground, trying to get some warmth. He turned to look for Holly – but she was gone.

Outside the secret alleys, a door slammed shut, and didn't open again.

Things had gone wrong before, but Holly had always been there, by his side. She was the one who knew what to do. And now she was gone.

A deep shudder of grief ran through him. There was a hole the shape of her inside his heart. It hurt, more than any wound he'd ever known.

Tam and Jess came over to him. They looked like

they'd been crying.

'You all right, Varjak?' said Tam softly, placing a paw on his flank.

He shook his head. He didn't want to talk.

'I know how you feel,' said Tam. 'I miss her too. More than anything.'

'And I miss my grandma,' said Jess.

Varjak's insides felt like snow. He could hardly meet their eyes. What could he tell them? *I was the one you were counting on – and I let you all down.*

'What happened to you back there, Varjak?' said Omar. 'It was like you started shimmering – and then you just quit! You didn't even try to fight Sally Bones!'

Varjak shivered. He could still feel the cold in his whiskers, the bruising in his brain as she entered his mind. 'I tried,' he said. 'But she – she was so strong.'

'No one can fight her,' mumbled Ozzie. 'Not even Varjak.'

The brothers looked beaten. 'We're finished,' said Omar. 'What are we going to do?'

'We're not finished!' said little Jess fiercely. 'I still think Varjak can beat Sally Bones. She's scared of him!'

'I don't think so,' said Tam. 'But something must have got to her, or we never would've escaped.'

Varjak shivered. All he could remember was the ice-blue eye, burning into his brain, freezing him to his core.

Outside the secret alleys, Cludge growled.

Tam went to the railings. 'The Scratch Sisters are out there!' she gulped. 'Cludge is holding them off, but they look so fierce! What should we do, Varjak?'

He joined her at the railings, and peered through to the alley outside. He saw Cludge backing away from the three Siamese cats: Elyza, Malisha and Pernisha Scratch. They were as lean and mean-looking as he remembered. Their claws glittered in the street light as they ghosted forwards through the rubble.

'Where is Varjak Paw?' demanded Elyza.

'We know he's here somewhere. Just tell us where, and we'll leave you alone.' She flashed her claws at Cludge, but he stood his ground bravely, and barked out another warning.

'*WOAH! WOAH!*'

'I hate those cats!' hissed Omar, clenching his paws. 'They think they're so great, but we're stronger than them, I know we are—'

'Let's fight them!' said Ozzie. Far in the distance, a siren wailed.

'No – you mustn't!' said Tam. 'What do we do, Varjak? I'm scared!'

Varjak's head hurt. It sounded like the Scratch Sisters were after him, too. He'd better be ready to fight. He took a deep breath and counted: in–two–three–four. He reached for his power –

– but there was ice in his belly.

Out—two—three—four –

Ice in his brain.

Come on, he told himself. Slow-Time, Moving Circles – I know how to do this.

In–two–three–four!

But there was only fear in his heart.

Out–two–three–four!

Sally Bones's ice-blue eye in his mind.

It felt like his lungs were shrinking. He couldn't breathe. He slumped to the ground, shaking, gasping for breath.

The power wasn't there any more.

It was gone.

Out in the alley, half a dozen cats crept up behind the Scratch Sisters. A patrol from Sally Bones's gang. Street lights flickered in the freezing wind. Their shadows danced on the walls. Cludge edged away from them, crouching low in the rubble.

'Well, look at this,' said the patrol leader. 'It's the Scratch Sisters. What do you think you're doing in the city centre?'

'Looking for Varjak Paw,' said Elyza Scratch.

'That cat's an outlaw. Sally Bones wants him, dead or alive. He's ours.'

Dead or alive, thought Varjak. What difference does it make any more? I've lost Holly, I've lost Mrs Moggs, and now I've lost the power. I've got nothing left. Absolutely nothing.

'If we find him, he's ours,' said Elyza Scratch. 'This is neutral ground.'

The patrol leader shook his head. 'Nothing's neutral now. These are our streets, and this is our law.'

'Our claws are the only law we know!' snarled Elyza. 'These streets have always been free for everyone.'

'Those days are over. The city belongs to our gang, and there's nothing you can do about it.'

Elyza's tail thudded in the rubble.
'Are you disrespecting the Scratch Sisters?'
she said menacingly.
'Because Scratch Sisters never,
ever back down.'

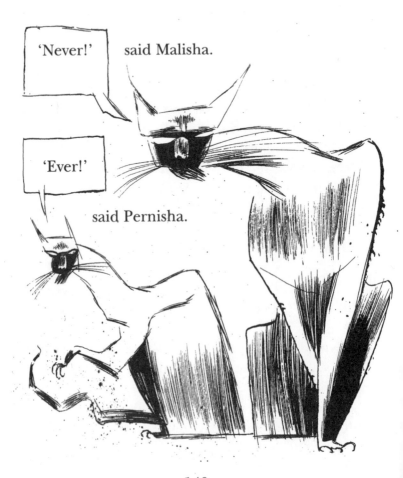

'Never!' said Malisha.

'Ever!'

said Pernisha.

They unsheathed their claws. Their pale green eyes narrowed to slits. They were out-numbered, but they knifed forwards, bristling at the Bones gang.

'Then it's time we taught you some manners!' snarled the patrol leader.

The two forces came together in a frenzy, fighting savagely on the street. Dust and debris swirled around them. Cludge kept well away, but the momentum of the fight was already taking them out of the alley. Watching behind bars, it seemed to Varjak that the Scratch Sisters were the better fighters – their claws flashed with stunning speed – but the Bones cats would win through sheer weight of numbers. Three of them swarmed all over a Scratch Sister, and she cursed violently; but they were gone

from view, round the corner, before he could see what happened next.

Tam groaned with relief. 'That was *so* close!'

'They'll be back,' said Omar. 'We've got to get out of here.'

'We can't leave the secret alleys!' cried Tam, her fur and whiskers ruffled. 'It's the only safe place – Holly always said so!'

'Well, it's not safe any more,' said Omar. 'We have to find somewhere else – right, Varjak?'

Varjak couldn't answer. It hurt too much, even hearing Holly's name.

Yet he knew Omar was right. They had to leave the secret alleys, or they'd be found, and then Holly's sacrifice would mean nothing. He didn't want to face the city streets again, without his power – but he couldn't give up now. I have to go on, he told himself. I have to find somewhere safe for us all. Because that's what Holly would do.

He slipped out through the railings to find Cludge. The big dog was hiding in the rubble, by an old cardboard box.

'Cludge scared!' he was muttering. 'Scary cats come back! Want to go!'

One by one, the others followed Varjak out of the secret alleys, into the winter afternoon. 'So it's true?' said Omar. 'You're really friends with a dog?'

'That's right,' said Varjak, huddling against the

cold. 'Cludge, these are our new friends: Omar and Ozzie, and Jessie.'

'Cludge!' barked the big dog. He wagged his tail at them. Jess smiled; but Omar and Ozzie's manes ruffled up.

'We can't go round with a dog!' said Omar. 'He'll give us away. Doesn't he know any other dogs? Doesn't he have a family?'

Cludge whimpered. Varjak frowned. Holly had once asked the same questions. Then, as now, Cludge had looked like a frightened puppy.

'Cludge is our friend,' said Tam. 'If he wants to come with us, he can come.'

'But it's dangerous,' said Omar, his eyes flashing. 'He's a *dog*, Tam!'

Varjak didn't like the way Omar was speaking. He could see confusion in Cludge's eyes; could see his great ears drooping. He turned on the stocky cat.

'Didn't you hear what Tam said? Cludge is our *friend* – and I'm not losing another one. He's not being left behind.'

Omar stared at Varjak – and then shrugged his rugged mane. 'Whatever,' he said.

'All right, Cludge?' said Tam. 'You're coming with us.'

The big dog grinned, and wagged his tail again. 'Friends!' he barked. 'Varjak and his friends!' He looked around. 'Where Holly go?'

143

Varjak opened his mouth to answer – but he couldn't. No words came out.

'She's somewhere else,' said Tam quietly. 'Now, where are we going?'

No one had an answer to that. As they stood there in silence, the wind dropped, and the city grew still. Daylight was fading. Soon it would be night again.

Jess cleared her throat. 'What about Grandma's tales?' she said. 'That secret city where it's always warm, and there's more mice than you can eat?'

A big smile crossed Ozzie's face. 'I've heard that tale,' he said. 'We heard it when we were kittens – remember, Omar?'

'I remember! But I don't know anyone who's been there, or even believes it.'

'Holly always believed it,' said Tam. 'And so did I, deep down . . . Did Mrs Moggs ever tell you where it was, Jessie?'

Jess shook her head. 'She just said there was fearsome guardians outside, so cats haven't been there for years—'

'Cludge know the place,' murmured Cludge. 'Bad place. Smelly.'

At first, Varjak thought he was joking. But Jess's eyes had lit up.

'That's right,' she breathed. '*The most disgusting smell you can imagine* – that's what Grandma said!'

'Do you really know this secret city, Cludge?' asked Varjak.

'No no no,' said Cludge, obviously regretting that he'd mentioned it. 'Not there. Not go back there—'

'Back?' said Varjak. 'You've been there before?' He looked deep into Cludge's eyes, and again saw a frightened puppy, who didn't want to go to a place that was clearly no joke. The sun was setting fast now. There wasn't much time left till nightfall. 'Cludge,' he said, 'if there's a place you know that cats never go – please take us there.'

Cludge shook his head. 'No, Varjak, no—'

'Please,' said Varjak. 'We need your help. It's important.'

Cludge looked at him. Then he looked away, eyes full of pain and fear and sadness.

'Please,' Varjak said again. 'Whatever's in that place, we'll face it together. You won't be alone, I promise.'

'Not alone?'

'Never.'

'Come, then,' sighed the big dog. 'Come with Cludge.'

Chapter Eighteen

Cludge led them away from the secret alleys, through the streets. It was night now, and the wind had dropped completely. Thick white mist descended on the city centre. It came right down to street level, where it crouched and coiled around the lamp posts, covering everything in damp, cold whiteness.

Visibility was low. They couldn't see far ahead through the mist. Sometimes Varjak smelled an unnatural, ghostly scent on the air, making his fur prickle. Sometimes he sensed the padding of paws, or the almost silent swish of claws.

Once, they heard rowdy voices, and ducked into a doorway just as a patrol of four cats from Sally Bones's gang came looming out of the mist. They had a wretched-looking Free Cat with them, an old tortoiseshell tom, and they were cuffing him around the head.

'But I wasn't doing nothing!' protested the tortoiseshell.

'You're harbouring outlaws!' said a Bones cat. 'Tell us where to find Varjak Paw, or you'll be an outlaw too – and we'll have your ears, and your tail, and then we'll rip out your whiskers, one by one—'

'But I don't know!' he shrieked, holding up his paws. 'No one knows!'

'You're either with us,' spat the Bones cat, 'or against us.' They hit him again, silencing him.

'I know that Free Cat!' whispered Jess, crouching in the doorway. 'He never hurt no one – we got to help him! Varjak, can't you—'

Varjak wished he could. He hadn't wanted the power before; it had only brought him trouble. Now it was gone, all he wanted was to have it back, to help his friends. But they had no idea he'd lost it. How could he tell them?

'It's too risky,' hissed Omar, before Varjak could say anything. 'Got to stay hidden.' The patrol passed from view and out of earshot, into the misty night.

Varjak and his friends came out of the doorway, very cautiously. The patrol was long gone now – but Varjak's Awareness was still tingling. Were they being watched? All he could see was the white mist, moving silent as roadkill; all he could smell was the ghost scent of cats, thick upon it. He thought he heard someone mewling.

'Who's there?' he called. 'Show yourself!'

'Varjak?' came a weary-sounding voice in the distance. 'Is that you?'

And through the crawling whiteness came Old Buckley, with a ragged column of Free Cats behind him. They looked exhausted, but they were all right; they didn't have Sally Bones's mark upon them. Jess ran up to them, and they nuzzled each other hard.

'Where's Grandma?' she asked Old Buckley.

His thin face crumpled up, though he tried not to show her. 'It was terrible, Jessie. Your grandma – she didn't make it. They got her. They got lots of us.' He shuddered. 'Sally Bones left before dawn. Said she'd be back tonight.'

Varjak's throat was tight. 'I'm sorry,' he said. 'I – I let everyone down.'

'No,' said Old Buckley. 'You was brave, trying to fight her. For a moment there, you gave us hope. But we never had a chance.'

'Where are the others?' said Jess.

'Hiding,' said Buckley. 'They don't want to be seen.' He began to choke. 'It's awful, Jessie, what she done.'

Varjak looked down. The city had become a place of horror. He couldn't stop the horror. He couldn't fight Sally Bones. But he could still help the Free Cats.

'If they're coming back, you can't stay here,' he said. 'Come with us. We're looking for Mrs Moggs's secret city.'

Old Buckley's troubled face broke up into a smile. 'Old Moggs,' he murmured. 'She loved a good tale.'

'It's no tale, Buckley!' said Jess. 'It's true. Cludge knows it!'

'Cludge?' He looked up and saw the dog for the first time, and arched his back in fear.

'It's all right!' said Jess. 'He's our friend – and he's taking us to the city. Come with us, Buckley – you got to. Grandma would come, if she was here . . .'

Old Buckley turned to his Free Cats. 'All right. You lot stay here. Stay safe. I'll come back and find you – if this place turns out to be real.' They melted back into the mist, as Buckley joined Varjak and the others.

Cludge led them on through the streets. They had to tread carefully, for anything could be hidden beneath the mist. The pavements were littered with smashed bottles and shards of glass. If only there were mice in there instead, thought Varjak as they walked. He was hungrier and colder than ever. Still, at least there was hope now; at least they were going somewhere.

But the further they travelled, the clearer it became that Cludge was leading them westwards: towards Sally Bones's territory.

'This is mad,' muttered Buckley. 'Following a dog, to a place that don't exist—'

'It does, too!' said Jess.

'Maybe it exists, maybe it doesn't,' said Omar. 'But why would a dog know it when we don't?'

'Don't be mean to Cludge!' said Tam. 'If you ever listened to him, you'd realize he always tells the truth. I was scared of him too at first – but now I'd follow him anywhere.'

Omar snorted. 'Never thought you were a dog-lover, Tam!'

'That's enough,' said Varjak. 'If you've got a better plan, let's hear it.'

'But we're just getting nearer to danger,' said Old Buckley. 'And—'

aa-wooooooooooooo

An eerie howl tore through the night, silencing them all. *Don't come here*, it seemed to say. *Turn back now and go away.* Varjak knew that sound. He'd heard it when they'd gone to rescue Jess.

'What's that smell?' whispered Tam.

Varjak sniffed the air. There was a disgusting stench wafting through the streets. And now Cludge was heading off the roadside,

151

down a slope, towards a concrete structure in the distance.

'There!' he barked, tail stiff with tension. 'There the place!'

'I don't believe it!' said Omar. 'Look where he's brought us! No one comes here – no one!'

Varjak's neck fur prickled, for Cludge had led them to the Storm Drain: the one place Holly had told him never to go. It was like a giant basin built of concrete, with rusting drainpipes and water towers along its banks. A stream of dark brown liquid ran through its centre.

At the far end of the Storm Drain, he could see a gateway. It was the entrance to a drainage tunnel, an open hole in the earth. The brown stream slopped around its mouth, through some rusty bars, and down into the hole. It was raw sewage. It stank.

A pack of dogs guarded this tunnel's mouth. Twenty dogs, maybe more. Big, fearsome-looking dogs, their teeth flecked with spit, their hides heaving. They sprawled by the stream of sewage like they owned it. Most of them were sleeping. One of them was howling at the moon. Then it laid down its head, closed its eyes, and started to snore – deep, resounding snores that echoed round the Storm Drain like a pneumatic drill.

'See?' murmured Cludge. 'Bad place. We go now?'

'Where's this city?' said Varjak.

'There is no city!' said Old Buckley. 'It's all make-believe and tales!'

Cludge shook his head. 'In hole,' he whispered. 'City under city.'

'City under city?' said Varjak. 'In hole?' And then it came together in his mind, like a light flickering on. 'You mean – the sewers?'

'Yah!' panted Cludge. 'No cats there. Stinking place.'

'You're not wrong,' said Tam, covering her nostrils with a paw. 'It's revolting! How can those dogs stand it?'

Cludge shrugged. 'Smells good to dogs. Smells sweet.' He sniffed the air with his wet black nose, breathed in deep – and then shook his head violently, and stopped sniffing. He looked small and scared again. 'But Cludge hate that smell now! Stinking, stinking, bad place!'

'It's gross,' muttered Omar. 'Can we go, Varjak?'

'No, this is it!' said Jess. Her blue eyes gleamed. 'Grandma was right, see? Fearsome guardians and a disgusting smell – but it'll be warm down there, and we'll be safe.'

Varjak nodded. 'Sally Bones's gang would never think of coming here.'

'Why would they?' said Old Buckley. 'If the stench don't kill you, them wild dogs will!'

'Oh, but they won't,' said Varjak, a plan forming

in his mind. 'Not if a dog talks to them for us.'

'This is insane,' said Omar.

Ozzie grimaced. 'It smells so bad.'

'It's up to you what you do,' said Varjak. 'I can't make anyone follow me. But that sewer is the safest place we could be.'

'Cats don't go down sewers!' cried Old Buckley.

'Cats can do anything,' said Varjak. 'Anything at all. No one thought I could talk to a dog – but I did, and now Cludge is my friend. This is the same. How about it, Cludge? Will you talk to those dogs for us, and explain that we need a place to hide?'

Cludge shivered. 'No, Varjak, bad dogs. Angry dogs. Not them. Please not—'

His eyes were clouding up again, worse than before. Varjak could see he wouldn't be able to persuade his friend. That meant there was only one thing for it. They needed a hiding place, and he was going to find them one – even if it meant facing a pack of wild dogs on his own. He didn't need his power to do this. Just courage.

'I am going to go down there and talk to those dogs,' he said, as calmly as he could. 'Cludge, if you're my friend, you'll come with me; I need you by my side. The rest of you, stay here till I call you.'

Varjak Paw didn't wait for answers. He set off into the Storm Drain on his own – towards the pack of sleeping dogs.

Chapter Nineteen

Varjak padded down the Storm Drain's concrete banks, and along the stream of sewage that ran through its middle. Ahead of him, the pack of sleeping dogs snored. Behind him, Cludge whined softly.

'But – scary dogs – bad place – come back, Varjak!'

Varjak walked on towards the dogs. With every step, the smell of sewage grew worse. It pricked the back of his nose. It made his eyes water.

'Go with him, Cludge!' he heard Tam say. 'If you don't, they'll tear him to pieces!'

Varjak followed the sewage. Still the dogs slept on. The stench was intense. He tried to close his nostrils and breathe through his mouth, but it made him cough –

cough cough

A dog shifted on its belly. Its yellow eyes opened – and then it saw him.

'WOAH! WOAH! WOAH!'

In a flash, the whole pack was up. Twenty dogs. All barking at Varjak. Snapping their teeth.

Keep going, Varjak told himself. Cludge won't let me down. He's my friend. He won't let me be torn to pieces by these dogs, they're about to rip me to pieces, they're going to bite my head off and – *stop thinking about it! Just keep going!*

The dogs came out to circle him. One of them reared up on its hind legs and thrashed the air around him with sledgehammer paws. Still there was no sign of Cludge.

The pack surrounded him, snarling wildly. Muscles and veins stood out on their necks. Their flanks heaved. The noise and stench were over-powering.

    i'm never going to make it
        they're going to tear me to bits
            this is it
                here i come, holly, here i come to join you,
                wherever you are –

– and then, from behind him, with a tremendous volley of barks, Cludge burst through the circle of dogs. He came crashing through them all to stand by Varjak's side.

'*CLUDGE!*' he barked. '*CLUDGE! CLUDGE! CLUDGE!*'

He silenced the pack. They stared at Varjak and Cludge, their eyes and jaws wide open.

Absolute silence in the Storm Drain.

'Cludge?' whispered the biggest, baddest-looking dog – a vast old silver hound, twice Cludge's size.

Cludge nodded. 'Cludge,' he said again.

Varjak stayed stock still as the silver hound lumbered out of the circle, and approached the two of them. The hound sniffed at Cludge, sniffed some more, and then sniffed again. His black eyes flickered. He turned to the pack, and nodded gravely.

'Cludge!' he declared, in a voice that rumbled like thunder, charged with a simple but immensely deep joy. 'Little Cludge!'

The dogs went wild. They rushed up to Cludge – sniffing, licking, yelping – all their anger gone. 'Cludge come back!' they barked. 'Cludge come back to dogs!'

Varjak blinked. 'You know these dogs?' he whispered.

'Cludge's family!' Cludge whispered back.

'But you said your family was angry with you—'

Cludge looked shyly up at the silver hound. 'Not angry, Pappa Dog?'

'Angry?' boomed the hound. 'With little Cludge? Dogs *miss* Cludge! Miss Cludge *so much*!'

And now Varjak understood what had happened. This was Cludge's family. This was his home. They'd had a quarrel, and he'd run away, believing he could never go back. But whatever the quarrel was about, it was long forgotten. The dogs were so happy to see him. They surrounded him with their warm bodies and wagging tails, and slowly, their happiness spread into Cludge himself, until it shone out of his clear black eyes, and lit him up with a pleasure Varjak had never seen before.

For the first time, he thought, Cludge looked like he really belonged somewhere. A dog alone in a world of cats was so much less than a dog surrounded by his pack of hounds. Holly was right to wonder about Cludge's family. Wasn't she always right?

Holly. The thought of her cut through him like winter wind. Would he ever get used to her not being there?

Cludge was flanked by a pair of magnificent black hounds now. They looked a lot like him – only they were bigger, older and stronger, like he might be one day. 'Varjak, look!' he yelped. 'Cludge's brothers! Buster and Bomballooloo!'

'Who the cat, Cludge?' said Buster, the dog on his left.

'Cats not come for years,' said Bomballooloo, the dog on his right.

'Varjak Paw,' Cludge told them. 'Cludge's friend. Helped Cludge when Cludge alone.'

'Cludge's friend?' they said. Varjak stood very still

as they sniffed him all over – and then covered him with warm, wet, friendly licks.

'Welcome, friend!' barked Buster.

'Friend brought Cludge back home!' barked Bomballooloo.

'How we thank you, Varjak Paw?' said Pappa Dog. 'What we do for you?'

Varjak smiled up at them. 'Well, there *is* something you can help us with,' he said. 'Is it true there's a city under the city, through that tunnel?'

'True,' said Pappa Dog. He pressed his face up to the bars of the gateway. 'Dark, empty place. Smells luvverly – but dogs too big to pass through.'

'Me and my friends, we need a place to hide,' said Varjak. 'Will you let us through, so we can hide in there?'

'Hide?' rumbled the huge hound. 'From who?'

'Sally Bones, the thin white cat,' said Varjak. He shivered. 'Our enemy.'

Pappa Dog drew himself up to his full height. 'Twenty dogs here,' he said. 'No one – *no one!* – get past twenty dogs. You, Varjak Paw, you and your friends, you get past. Thin white cat – never.' He spoke with great solemnity, in a voice that seemed as old and strong as the earth itself.

'Thank you, Pappa Dog,' said Varjak. He turned to the top of the Storm Drain, and nodded at his friends to come down. The mist was parting.

159

Through it, he could see a clear night sky up above, and a full moon shining bright.

One by one, they came out into the open and joined him. The dogs stood back to let them through. If only Holly could see this, he thought. A gang of cats, walking past a pack of dogs, with nothing but friendship and respect on either side.

'Cludge want to come,' said Cludge, 'but – Cludge's pack – been so long—'

Varjak didn't want to leave him either, after all they'd been through together; but Cludge looked so happy here at last, with Pappa Dog, and Buster and Bomballooloo, and all the rest of them.

'It's all right, my friend,' said Varjak. 'I think this is your place, with your pack. But thank you for saving us – again.'

'Var . . . Jak,' murmured Cludge, licking him gently. 'You need dogs, you call. We come.'

'Thank you, Cludge. And we'll be there for you, too.'

'Friend,' said Cludge. 'Cludge your friend for ever!'

They parted then; and Varjak turned to Tam and Jess, to Omar and Ozzie and Old Buckley. He led them forwards through the gateway: into the tunnel, into the darkness, into the city under the city.

Chapter Twenty

There was a stream of sewage in the centre of the tunnel. There was no way round it. Varjak put a paw down into the thick, brown stream. It was sloppy and sticky. It stank to the skies.

He pulled his paw out. It was covered in slime. He tried to close his nostrils and breathe through his mouth, but now he could taste it as well as smell it. He wanted to retch.

'Keep going, Varjak,' said Jess, behind him. 'It won't all be like this. Grandma used to say it was well hidden; you had to go a way to get there.'

Varjak nodded. What was the choice, with Sally Bones and her gang at large? Compared to her ice-blue eye, even sewage seemed inviting. He plunged his paw back in again, and squelched forwards through the nauseating wetness.

It was dark in there. It got darker with every step. The air grew closer, warmer, as they went further in. Soon it was so dark, Varjak couldn't see any more.

He could only feel the sewage, splashing his fur. It was oozing into his skin, bubbling around his legs, getting deeper all the time.

He kept walking. It felt like he was going down-hill, down into the bowels of the earth. The stream sloshed up around him, soaking the fur on his belly.

'Stop!' cried Old Buckley. 'I can't go no further! I'm going to be sick!'

'It'll change,' said Jess.

'Even if it does,' grunted Omar, 'Cludge was right. This is a bad place, Varjak.'

Varjak kept going. He was thinking about a room with no light. *What seems true at one moment may not be true the next.*

'We've come this far,' he said aloud. 'I hate it too, but we can't stop now.'

He tried to sound confident – for Jess, for them all – but he didn't feel so certain. The river of sewage just seemed to be getting deeper. They were going further and further down, and it was hard to imagine how it could ever change.

Every step brought the brown stream higher. Now the slime was crawling up his neck, its rancid stickiness reaching his throat, almost up to his mouth, and still there was no light, and Varjak began to imagine being swept away on a tide of stinking sewage, drowning in brown slime –

– and then his paw came down short; and his

163

next paw came down shorter. Steps! He'd found some steps! He climbed up them, fast as he could. With a sucking, squelching sound, his body came clear away from the sewage, and he was standing on another level, above the stream.

It was still darker than the darkest city night, but far overhead, he could see faint shafts of amber light. With a jolt, he realized they came from street lights, filtering into the sewers through those grilles in the ground. They'd come so far underground, the street seemed as high above them as the sky.

He looked down again. Below, he could see the stream of sewage flowing through the middle of the tunnel. Either side of it, there were elevated platforms, like pavements either side of a road. He was standing on one of these. It was warm and dry, and it stretched far off into the distance. He could make out some kind of chamber up ahead, and more tunnels beyond, like passages or alleyways.

His heart lightened at the sight. Mrs Moggs's tales were true! It was a whole city under the city. A secret city. And no one would ever find them here.

One by one, his friends squelched out of the sewage, up the stairs to join him. The platform was broad enough for them all. They were filthy and sopping wet. They stood there, shaking foul liquid from their fur.

'Mudcats,' muttered Tam. 'We've turned into mudcats.'

'Who cares?' said Varjak. 'Let's explore!'

They set off again. Soon the tunnel widened out, and they came to an underground cavern. It was made of elaborately glazed brickwork, shiny and beautiful even in the dimness. Its walls curved up smoothly, meeting in a dome. Many tunnels and streams crossed here. Varjak could see them radiating out in every direction. This was a whole world in itself – and they were the only ones in it.

Old Buckley was looking around, wonder in his eyes. 'It's incredible,' he said. 'Moggs's tales was true!'

'And there's mice here!' said Jess. 'Can you hear 'em, Buckley? Can you?'

She was right. Varjak sensed them: warm, fresh, juicy mice. Lots of them.

So this was where they came in winter! Thanks to Cludge, thanks to Mrs Moggs and her tales, he'd found them at last. And they were free for any cat to hunt. No unfair laws down here. No Sally Bones. He smiled, and let out a low howl that echoed round the cavern, rippling the underground river that ran through it.

'What now?' said Omar.

'Three guesses,' said Tam. 'Who wants mouse for supper? Fearless Tam's going hunting!'

'And I'm coming with you!' laughed Omar.

'Me too,' said Ozzie, joining in. 'The Orrible Twins—'

'No, little brother,' said Omar. 'You wait here. We'll bring you something good.'

Ozzie blinked. 'But – but I'm hungry too.'

'You can stay with Varjak,' said Omar. 'Me and Tam, we're a hunting team.'

Varjak watched them with a pang in his heart. That was how he felt about Holly. They were a team. Who'd hunt with him now? He felt sorry for Ozzie, too. The big cat wanted to go with his brother; but it was clear that Omar and Tam wanted to be alone.

'Come on, Ozzie,' said Jess. 'Come with me. Let's explore – we might find something better than mice.'

'Nothing's better than mice,' grumbled Ozzie, but he let Omar and Tam go.

'You come too, Varjak,' said Jess. 'And you, Buckley.'

Old Buckley shook his head. 'I'm going to rest,' he said. 'And then I'm going back to find the Free Cats, and bring 'em down here.'

Varjak, Jess and Ozzie headed further into the sewers, through caverns and along platforms lit only by those faint shafts of light. They travelled in a straight line westwards, going deeper all the time. It got warmer as they went. Varjak thought it was probably always warm down here. Why would the weather ever change? Up on the streets, it could be snowing, or windy, or storming, and he'd never know.

He felt a glow of satisfaction. This was a fine place to hide.

As they walked on westwards, the platform started to slope up again. Varjak guessed they were coming back towards the surface. He could hear the stream of sewage in the tunnel getting stronger, faster, gathering pace. Its level was rising, too.

Before long, they came to the end of the platform. A series of steps led back into the frothy brown sewage. Far in the distance, Varjak thought he saw daylight, but couldn't be sure.

'We must be under Sally Bones's territory,' said Jess. 'We been going west long enough.'

Sally Bones's territory. Varjak remembered it from the night they'd rescued Jess: the river and the railway bridge, and that churning brown froth on the water –

Churning brown froth?

'Maybe that's where the sewers come out into the river!' he said.

'Yup,' said Ozzie. 'That brown stuff we saw.'

Varjak nodded. Ozzie wasn't as slow as he looked. He was a cat of few words, and Varjak had never thought too much about him, taking him for granted as a fighting machine. But now he wondered what else went on in Ozzie's mind, what the big cat felt, what his dreams were like.

'Well, this is as far as we can go without swimming in sewage again,' Varjak said out loud. 'Let's get back and see how the hunting went.'

They returned to the central cavern. Old Buckley was curled asleep, snoring loud as any dog. Omar and Tam were giggling. They were in high spirits. They had a heap of mice laid out before them.

'Look what we found!' boasted Tam.

'Yum,' said Jess as they settled down to eat.

Varjak crunched into a mouse. Its juices squirted in his mouth. The rich flavours sang on his tongue. It was good. It was better than good: there was no taste like it. He ate it fast, and then a second one, and then a third.

His face felt warm, and he was filled with the pleasure of food for the first time since . . . since . . . since he and Holly had feasted in the harbour yard. Black-and-white fur mixing into silver-blue. Starlight strong between them –

No.

There was no point thinking about that. It was a lifetime ago, and now it was gone. This was his life now. This underworld. This city under the city. This sewer.

He curled up in the darkness, on his own, and went to sleep.

Chapter Twenty-one

Down in the sewers, Varjak dreamed.

He dreamed he was back in Mesopotamia. He was in the ruined temple, by the clear blue pool that was the river's source. The whisker-thin window glowed with sunlight. The chamber smelled of mint.

Jalal sat beside him, looking into the pool. 'Think of a question,' said Jalal. 'Hold it in your mind. Keep looking at this pool long enough – and you will see the truth.'

Varjak didn't want to. What if the pool showed Jalal that he'd lost his power? What would his ancestor think of that? All Jalal's teaching, his training: it had all been for nothing.

But Jalal kept looking at the pool, so Varjak did too. He thought about Sally Bones. Was he really safe from her at last?

At first, he could only see himself, reflected back in the mirror-clear pool. But then the water seemed to flicker. It seemed to blur at the edges and grow thin, and just below its surface, Varjak saw an image taking shape, coming closer.

He saw a mountain. The white peak of a mountain. A narrow rock ledge, on that snow-capped peak. He recognized it now. It was the very mountain they were standing inside. He was looking at a peak he hadn't yet climbed. He smiled. This was surely a good sign. Maybe it meant he was going to get his power back, and everything would be OK, after all.

And then his blood froze. Because standing on top of the mountain peak was a thin white cat with an ice-blue eye.

Sally Bones.

Varjak gasped, and pulled away from the pool. 'She's here!' he cried. 'She's on top of the mountain!'

'Who?'

'Sally Bones! Can't you see her?'

Jalal looked into the pool. 'We each see what is most important to us,' he said. 'I see my old enemy. Did I ever tell you about her? Saliya of the North. She was the perfect warrior. None could beat her. Many tried, but no one could lay a paw on her. It seemed she might live for ever. She gave me my greatest battle.'

Varjak's pulse sped up. He remembered, long ago, his grandfather once mentioned Jalal's greatest battle – but Varjak had never heard the tale. Of course, Jalal would have won that battle. Jalal always won.

But Varjak was no Jalal. And now he'd seen a vision of Sally Bones in Mesopotamia. Even in his dreams, there was no escape.

'What do I do, Jalal?' he said. 'How do I beat my enemy?'

'Sometimes, my son, you cannot beat your enemy.' Varjak flinched at the words. He was certain now: Jalal knew he'd lost to Sally Bones. Once again, he felt the shame of defeat, stinging him. 'It depends where you fight, and when, and how,' Jalal went on. 'It depends on your strengths, and your enemy's weaknesses.'

'Weaknesses?' said Varjak. 'How can you know someone's weaknesses?'

'Like anything else. You *see* them. Face your enemy and see them truly, without fear, without hate. Only then can you know them.'

Face Sally Bones, again? Varjak turned away from the pool, shaking his head. Thanks for nothing, Jalal, he thought. Sometimes I wish I'd never come to Mesopotamia.

The light in the chamber started to fail. The window in the wall grew dimmer and dimmer, until once again, Varjak Paw stood in darkness.

Chapter Twenty-two

In the days and nights that followed, Old Buckley brought a trickle of Free Cats down to the sewers. Many had Sally Bones's mark upon them. They were a pitiful sight, even in the underground half-light.

'Don't look at us,' one of them said, covering his face. 'They took everything what made us cats. Please don't look.'

'That's not true!' protested Jess, leading them to food and water. 'We're still Free Cats. They can never take that from us.'

All the Free Cats who made it to the sewers told the same story. They said it was murder in the city. Sally Bones had returned to the centre at nightfall. The bloodshed was worse than before. Everyone was hiding, but one by one, they were being hunted down like prey and punished.

Their tales made Varjak shudder with pity, and with fear of Sally Bones. He was gladder than ever that he'd found this safe place. It was so far underground, nothing could reach them here: not the wind or snow, not the thin white cat. It was safe and warm, and there was plenty to eat. Sometimes he could almost convince himself that he was getting used to the smell.

But another part of him felt a smouldering anger rise. A sense of injustice burned within him. Sally Bones had to be stopped! Yet who could possibly stop her?

He shook his head. There's nothing I can do, he told himself. I tried, and I failed. I haven't got the power any more. It's gone.

One day, Old Buckley came down to the cavern with some cats Varjak didn't expect to see. Three lean, mean Siamese. The Scratch Sisters, walking tall as ever, knifing towards him through the gloom. Varjak's heart thudded in his throat. Old Buckley had brought the Scratch Sisters into the safety of the sewers!

'Varjak,' gulped Buckley. 'I ran into them, up on the streets. They got things to say, so I – I brought them down – no choice—'

Varjak stood up to meet them. Elyza and Malisha came first; Pernisha lurked in the shadows behind them. Their eyes were like points of pale green fire in the dimness. Their claws glittered, sharp and deadly. He could hear water dripping, echoing, running underground.

His paws tensed up. Why were they here? Beside him, Omar and Ozzie bristled. Malisha and Pernisha bristled right back. The tension was thick as the stench of sewage.

But Elyza greeted him like they were old friends. 'Varjak Paw! You've become a famous outlaw since we met.'

'So what?' said Varjak, keeping his guard up.

'Respect the Scratch Sisters when we talk to you!' snapped Malisha.

'Respect!' echoed Pernisha, still lurking behind them, out of sight.

'Don't tell us what to do,' growled Omar.

'Omar and Ozzie,' said Elyza. 'What trouble are you two making now?'

'You want trouble?' said Omar. His eyes flared dangerously, and big Ozzie stuck out his barrel chest. 'We'll give you trouble – no one's stronger than us!'

'You might be strong,' Elyza shot back, 'but no one's quicker than the Scratch Sisters. We'll cut your throats before you can move!' She flashed her claws at Omar – and then she laughed, and turned back to Varjak. 'But you can relax, Paw. We didn't come here to argue. We came to talk about *you*. Because you're the cat who fights like Sally Bones.'

Varjak felt ice in his belly. Elyza didn't know he'd lost the power. No one did. 'What about it?' he said, playing for time.

'Where's your friend Holly?' said Elyza. 'I always respected her. She's clever and brave – almost good enough to be a Scratch Sister.'

'She – she's – Sally Bones's gang got her.'

'That's what we heard,' said Elyza. 'So what are you doing about it?'

'Doing? We're staying alive—'

'You're hiding from the Bones, is what you're doing! They killed your best friend, and you're hiding in the sewers like a rat!'

Varjak clenched his paws tight. 'What else can we do?' he said. 'I can't beat Sally Bones – no one can!'

'We heard different,' said Malisha.

'We heard you got to her,' said Pernisha.

'We heard you found some weakness in the Bones,' said Elyza, 'and you escaped!'

Varjak looked up. He could see moisture glistening on the ceiling, dripping down the walls, flowing steadily into the stream of sewage. 'It's true we escaped,' he said at last. 'But I didn't find any weakness.'

Elyza's ears flicked forward. 'No one escapes from Sally Bones! We've been searching for her weakness for years, and we never found it! What did you do? How did you beat her?'

'I didn't beat her. I tried – and I failed.'

'That's not good enough,' said Elyza. 'You have to try and try again. You're the first cat who ever found her weakness – and you're throwing it away like a coward.'

'But we're safe down here,' said Varjak.

'Safe?' spat Elyza. 'No one's safe! Me and my Sisters, we came looking for you. We ran into a Bones patrol. We beat them, but see what happened first?'

Varjak looked closer at the Scratch Sisters. Pernisha was still lurking behind the others, in the shadows.

'Go on, Pernisha,' said Elyza, sharpening her claws.

'Don't want to,' muttered Pernisha.

'I said, go on! Show him what they did to you!'

Pernisha Scratch stepped forwards – and the fur on Varjak's neck prickled, for he realized why she'd been hiding. She only had one ear. The other had been ripped away.

'Sally Bones has gone too far!' thundered Elyza. 'No one does this to a Scratch Sister and gets away with it! She has to be stopped. We'd do it ourselves, only we can't touch her. We're the fastest claws in town, but she – she's the only one who knows that secret way of fighting.' She looked at Varjak, eyes gleaming like fire. 'But you can do it, Paw. You can beat Sally Bones. You're the only one!'

'Beat her!' said Malisha.

'Take her down!' said Pernisha. 'Do it for Holly!'

The anger in Varjak's heart blazed up. Do it for Holly. For a moment, he almost believed he could. They were that convincing.

But they were wrong.

'I'm sorry,' he said. 'I wish I could. But I can't fight her. I'm through with fighting.'

Tam spoke up. 'I was there in the yard too, when we escaped from Sally Bones,' she said. 'Whatever you did to her, Varjak, it wasn't about fighting. It was something else. It happened when she was looking into your eyes.'

'That's true,' said Jess. 'And you'd do it again, if you saw her – course you would!'

'But I don't even know what I did!' he protested.

'Anyway, it's not so easy,' said Omar. 'How would he get close enough to try?'

'You have to go to her place,' said Elyza. 'You have to go right up to that graveyard where she lives. It won't be easy. A cat can't do it alone. So you, Omar, and your brother Ozzie, and your friends – you have to help Varjak get there.'

'There aren't enough of us,' said Omar. 'Not for something like that.'

'That's why we're coming with you,' said Elyza. 'We know how dangerous it is. Those who go to Sally Bones's territory don't come back. But they ripped my sister's ear off. They disrespected us all. And for that, they will pay. We will fight to our last breath – because Scratch Sisters never, *ever* back down.'

Omar's eyes narrowed. 'You'd fight on our side? No tricks?'

'For a chance of vengeance,' whispered Pernisha, 'we would fight beside you, all the way.'

Omar nodded slowly, taking it in. 'That might be enough. It'll be hard – but we'll do our best, Varjak. We'll get you right up to Sally Bones, to give you the chance to face her again. Because what she's doing isn't right. And you might not be sure of yourself – but it's the only hope we've got.'

'Yup,' said big Ozzie stoutly. 'Count me in.'

Varjak was torn. They were brave, and so were the Scratch Sisters. But Sally Bones – her ice-blue eye burning into his brain – to face her again, on her own territory . . .

'You're mad!' cried Old Buckley. 'There's patrols all along the borders of Sally Bones's territory – you'll never get past them!'

'We don't have to,' said big Ozzie. 'The sewers come out deep inside her territory. We can get past the border without them even knowing.'

Omar's eyes widened. He flexed his powerful paws. 'Let's do it! Let's go now!'

Varjak turned to Tam and Jess, half hoping they'd put a stop to this, half hoping they wouldn't.

Tam coughed. 'Old Buckley's right,' she began.

'This is mad. It's stupid. I don't like it; it scares me stiff. But remember when we were hiding in the crate, Varjak? Remember the things Holly said then? Well, if you're going, I – I guess I'm coming with you. Because it's just the kind of mad, stupid plan Holly would dream up – and she'd never let you go alone!'

Everyone stared at Tam.

Then Omar laughed: a rich, warm laugh that echoed round the sewers, easing the tension. 'So it's true!' he said. 'You really are fearless, Tam!'

'And I'm coming too,' said Jess. 'Because my grandma, she believed in a free city for Free Cats. She believed Varjak was the one to make it happen. And she – she died, so we'd have a chance to do this. You know she did, and Holly did too . . .'

That was it. In his mind, Varjak saw again that terrible moment when Holly fell into the void, as he screamed her name, over and over and over again.

'All right,' he said. It was like someone else was talking, someone braver and stronger than him. 'I'll do it. I don't know what I'm supposed to do – but get me to Sally Bones again, and I swear: I will do my best to beat her.'

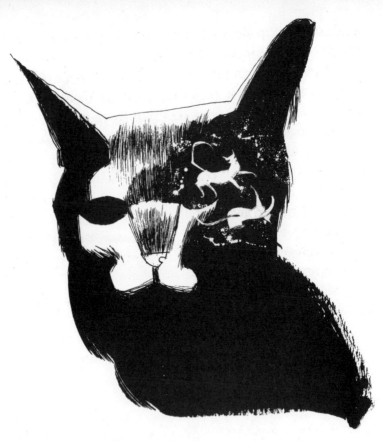

Chapter Twenty-three

They set off without further discussion, leaving Old Buckley and the Free Cats behind. Varjak looked at Tam and Jess, Omar and Ozzie, and the Scratch Sisters as they walked. He had only seven allies, against the whole of Sally Bones's gang. It wasn't much – but he was glad to have them.

They made their way in silence through the sewers, along dark tunnels, and up to the point where Varjak, Ozzie and Jess had been before – the point of no return. He stood on the edge of the platform, looking down into the stream of sewage. He could hear it roaring past; he could smell it, in all its stinking wetness. A series of steps led back into the churning brown froth.

'Here we go again,' he said. He held his breath and padded down the steps, into the sewage. He felt it slop up his paws, his legs, his belly –

'Ugh!' spat Malisha Scratch, behind him. 'This is disgusting!'

'Revolting!' said Pernisha.

'And dangerous!' said Elyza. 'Why's the current so strong, Paw?'

She was right. The stream felt much swifter here than at the entrance to the sewers. And the level was rising. The sound of the flow was getting louder: a rushing, crushing, whooshing sound that filled Varjak's ears and would have made his fur prickle, if it hadn't been plastered down with slime.

'I don't like this,' said Tam. 'I'm scared!'

'It's all right,' said Varjak, trying to give her courage. 'We can't be far from the river. It won't be long.'

He kept going, and they followed him; but there seemed to be no end to it. The level was rising, rising all the time. The sewage was up around his neck, and it wasn't just sticky slop any more. It was a hard, fast current that pressed against him like a force of nature. He was in deeper than ever, and it was all he could do to keep upright.

Without warning, the ground beneath his paws gave way. There was no ground any more. He was in free-fall, suspended in the stream, and it was the stream that was moving him along: he was out of control. He kicked with his back legs, trying to steer himself away from the tunnel walls, for if he hit them at this speed, it would knock him out. But even his strongest kick was nothing to the force of the flow.

The tunnel curved round suddenly, in a violent bend, and Varjak felt his insides come loose.

'Watch out!' he yelled; but his mouth filled with sewage the instant he opened it. The stream sloshed over his nose, his eyes, his ears.

It was a torrent now, and Varjak was lost in it. He was at its mercy – him and all his friends. He heard Tam scream behind him. Saw Ozzie, the strongest of them, swept up ahead of him, head over paws. The sewage turned him upside down. Varjak gulped a breath of air. He kicked and clawed, panic rising, rising.

They hit another bend, and were swept round a corner at terrifying speed. As he rounded it, Varjak saw an arc of light, curving crescent-shaped above him, like the moon.

It was the mouth of the sewer. The exit. The end. He was flung through it with tremendous force: hurled bodily out of the sewers, and finally into the river.

The water felt hard as concrete as he hit it. Stunned, gasping for breath, he kicked out with all his force – but the water here was shallow. His paws touched down easily on the river bed. He stood up. He was shaking all over; he was battered and bruised – but he was safe.

Behind him, a torrent of sewage frothed into the river, shooting out a stream of soaking wet cats. Varjak saw them spat out, bewildered, from the darkness into daylight.

He blinked. It was daytime. The light hurt his eyes. The winter wind whipped into his face. But he grinned. They'd made it. This is it, he thought. I'm back in my city!

He looked around. He wasn't far from the riverbank where he'd once fought Luger and the rest. High above, he could see the railway bridge. Further down river was a road bridge. On the opposite bank, he could see those great glass towers, reaching up to the sky. In among them, the smoke-dark tower of the graveyard. Sally Bones's place.

One by one, Varjak and the others hauled themselves out of the river and onto the muddy bank. They were deep behind enemy lines. They were in Sally Bones's territory, and Sally Bones knew nothing of it.

Varjak shook the water and sewage from his fur. It was freezing cold. His paws were numb. Snow lay thick on the ground. It was tight-packed, as if it had lain there for days and it might never be warm enough to melt. He kept looking over to the other side of the river, to that single, solitary tower of darkness. It was as if it was beckoning to him. Sally Bones's place.

'I can't swim this river,' said Tam, teeth chattering. 'I can't swim at all.' She looked like a drowned rat. 'Let's go back, we're never going to make it.'

'I can't swim either,' said Omar. 'But we don't have to. We'll cross the bridge—'

'Which bridge?' said Elyza Scratch, shaking out great showers of liquid. 'We'll never make it over the road bridge, it'll be too heavily guarded. The railway bridge won't be – but only because no cat in their right mind tries to cross a railway bridge.'

Omar grinned, and his eyes flashed. 'Who said we were in our right minds? We're going to Sally Bones's place! What's a little railway bridge,

compared to that?'

No one spoke for a moment. Then Varjak nodded. 'Good point,' he said.

Elyza Scratch glared at the Twins. 'You've got more muscles than brains, Omar. You always were a trouble-maker. Never had any respect.'

'Respect,' said Omar, 'is something you have to earn.'

'Is that a challenge?' Elyza and her Sisters unsheathed their deadly claws. The Twins stuck out their big, strong chests. The two groups faced each other, neither backing down, as the wind lashed the water, making it churn and seethe even more.

'What's wrong with you all?' said Varjak. 'We've got enough to worry about without fighting each other! Now come on.'

Neither group backed down – but they looked away from each other, and followed him. The confrontation was over. For now.

Chapter Twenty-four

Varjak and his allies padded up the riverbank, dripping wet. They climbed onto the pavement. The sky was darkening. It looked empty and hollow. There was no sun up there. No moon. No stars.

Before them now was a huge main road. On the other side of the road loomed the railway bridge. Around it, there were black iron street lamps, with monstrous carvings of fish coiled round them.

'Nice,' said Tam, shivering. '*Ah-ah-atchooo!*' She sneezed. 'This is miserable – we're filthy and soaking and I'm scared! I want to go back! I wish Cludge was here . . .'

'Don't worry, Fearless Tam,' said Omar.

'Stop calling me that! I never was fearless! I don't even like crossing roads this big!'

Cars, buses and trucks roared past in continuous flow. Their headlights were blinding, their exhaust fumes choking. There were no gaps in the traffic. The road was too dangerous to cross; but there was

an underpass running beneath it to the other side. Varjak headed down there. The others followed.

The underpass was full of rusty metal bins. It was lit only by a red strip light on the ceiling. There were puddles on the ground, giving off sharp, acrid odours. The red light buzzed with electric tension as they entered; and Varjak's heart skipped a beat, for at the other end of the underpass, there was a patrol from Sally Bones's gang.

Oh no, he thought. Not already.

Varjak and his friends took cover behind a bank of bins. From there, he watched the Bones patrol. There were five of them: big, battle-scarred cats, gathered around something at the far end, taking turns to kick it. It looked like a bloody heap of bones and fur; something barely alive.

But then its scent reached him: the ghostly scent of a cat with no ears or tail. It raised its head and hissed at the Bones patrol, the desperate hiss of a cat with nowhere left to go.

'Don't you hiss at us!' they spat, as they hit it again. 'You're nothing any more! You're not even a cat!'

'I – I was your captain. You can't do this!' croaked the cat. Varjak's fur prickled, for he knew that voice. It was Razor. The tiger-striped tomcat had been beaten beyond endurance; his ears and tail had been ripped off; but it was Razor, and he was in terrible trouble.

'We can do anything we like to you, Razor,' said the patrol leader. 'You're not in our gang any more.'

'I'd rather be in Varjak Paw's gang!' groaned Razor, as their claws cut him. 'At least he never slashed me – not like *her*!'

'We'll get that outlaw in the end,' said the leader. 'And he'll look just as pretty as you, when the Boss gets through with him.'

They all laughed. In his hiding place, Varjak's scalp prickled. He was feeling something he never thought he'd feel. He felt sorry for Razor. The big cat had been so cocky, so sure of himself. Now all his pride and power was stripped from him. Cowering in the rubbish, without his ears and tail, Razor looked pitifully naked. He was still hissing, trying to fend them off with the last of his strength, but he didn't stand a chance – unless someone stepped in to help.

'That cat needs back-up!' whispered Varjak.

'No!' shivered Tam. 'Don't do it.'

'Why not? There's five of them, but there's more of us.'

'Maybe, but this is only the beginning.' Tam bit her paws and frowned. 'We're never going to make it to Sally Bones's place at this rate – there aren't enough of us.'

Varjak shook his head. 'Razor needs help.' As the patrol closed in to finish Razor off, Varjak readied himself for action.

'Don't even think about it, Paw!' hissed Elyza Scratch. 'That scum's not worth it.'

'Razor's not so bad,' said Ozzie, speaking up. 'He's a show-off, but I always kind of liked him.'

Omar nodded. 'Stay back, Varjak,' he commanded. 'We'll handle this. Come on, little brother! Yee-haa!' Ozzie grinned. The Orrible Twins shoved Varjak out of the way, and sprang towards the patrol.

Stay back, Varjak? What did Omar mean, stay back? There were five in the patrol – did Omar think they could beat five cats, all on their own? Or did he suspect that Varjak had lost the power?

Normally, Varjak wouldn't have thought twice. He'd feel confident if he could drop into Slow-Time, if he could make a Moving Circle, if he could feel the energy rising up inside him. But without it . . .

He watched Omar and Ozzie go first. He heard their ferocious growls as the brothers barrelled into the fight. Omar lashed out at the leader, and drew blood. Beside him, Ozzie's mighty swing erupted all over the patrol.

But the Bones cats were tough. They weren't scared of the Twins. They hit right back. One of them cracked Omar across the face.

Varjak couldn't watch. He couldn't stand by and see his friends, out-numbered, take a beating. Maybe he didn't have the power any more, but he was going to help.

193

He strode into the dark red dimness. 'Takes five of you to beat Razor, does it?' he growled. 'Let's see what you can do in a fair fight.'

The Bones cats drew back. 'It's him!' they hissed. 'The outlaw Varjak Paw!'

Razor's scar-torn face lit up. 'Varjak?' he whispered.

'Stay back!' panted Omar. 'I told you, we'll handle this.'

But Varjak's pride was stung. He breathed deep, reached for the power –

in–two–three–four; out–two–three–four

– and it all started again in his mind, like a nightmare coming back, a nightmare from which there was no escape:

Sally Bones's ice-blue eye, burning into his brain –

– the darkness –

– the despair –

– *can't breathe* –

'Look out!' cried Omar.

The patrol leader swung at Varjak. Omar tried to get in the way, but the leader got there first.

CRACK!

His big, hard paw smashed into Varjak's face. Varjak's legs went weak. His head was on fire. He had no power. He couldn't fight back. The leader was so much bigger, so much stronger. Without the power, he felt naked and empty as the sky.

CRACK!

CRACK!

CRACK!

Ultra-violet pain exploded in his head. The side of his face felt wet. Varjak looked up, dazed. In the dim red light, he saw the Scratch Sisters, coming out to fight. Behind them, Tam was biting her paws, frowning – and then, suddenly, Tam turned. She turned tail. She sprinted back down the underpass, back the way they'd come.

'Tam!' he called. She didn't even look round, she was running so fast. The last thing he saw was her bushy tail, disappearing.

She was gone. Tam had run away.

CRACK!

The patrol leader hit him once more. He slammed Varjak's body, flinging him at the bins. Varjak crashed into them, head on. The metal groaned with the impact

and everything

everything

every

thing

stopped

Chapter Twenty-five

Varjak dreamed. He dreamed of the salty sea air. Salty? Sea air?

Before him, sparkling blue and brilliant, was the sea. He was standing on sand, soft beneath his paws. An ocean breeze played upon his face. Waves rolled in with a gentle hushing sound, like the wind through a million leaves, and then they rolled out again. In and out, in and out; the waves came and went, endless; and Varjak thought he'd never felt so peaceful, so serene. Seagulls wheeled and turned on their wingtips through the sky. High above, behind the sea, he could see the mountains, with their perfect white peaks.

The water looked so lovely. It wasn't like the waters of the real world. It was warm gentle water that would carry him for ever and ever. He was filled with the desire to dip into the tide, and wade out to sea.

'No further!' said a voice behind him. 'It is not your time, Varjak Paw.'

Varjak turned. It was his ancestor. 'Where are we, Jalal?' he said.

The old cat smiled, not without sadness. 'This? This is the sea, my son. Where all rivers end.'

'It's beautiful.'

'It is. But it is not for you. Not yet.'

Varjak looked up at the sky. The sun was setting. Its final rays sank beneath the horizon.

'Oh!' said Varjak. 'I think I understand.'

Jalal smiled. 'You are learning how to see, at last. Now you must go back where you belong, and do what you must do.'

'I don't think I'll ever be ready for that,' sighed Varjak. 'I can't fight her, Jalal. I can't even look her in the eye.'

'I know,' said Jalal quietly. 'The same happened to me with Saliya of the North.'

'What? But – but you're the great Jalal!'

'Well, the great Jalal lost his greatest battle. No matter how good you are, there is always someone better.'

'But *you* can't lose a fight! You know everything!'

Jalal's amber eyes sparkled. 'No one knows everything. Not even Jalal the Paw! No one is unbeatable. Everyone has a weakness. I did not find my enemy's – yet she had one, too. And I knew that some day, a cat would come who *could* find it, and put an end to her reign of darkness. Perhaps a cat like you, my son.

Perhaps a cat like you.'

Jalal looked away, into the horizon. The sun had set. It was dark now over the sunless sea. 'Never give up,' he said. 'Remember: one ray of light can change everything. And Varjak Paw?'

'Yes, Jalal?'

'Keep the Way alive.'

Chapter Twenty-six

Varjak opened his eyes. The sea was gone. Above his head, a red strip light buzzed. He was back in the underpass, sprawled by the bins, in an acrid-smelling puddle. His face felt like raw meat. His friends were around him, looking worried.

'Varjak?' said Omar. 'Can you hear me? Are you OK?'

'I'm fine,' he said, though his head ached, and his body was sore.

'You must have nine lives!' breathed Jess. 'We thought you was finished there.'

Varjak coughed. There was blood on his fur. Did they know he'd lost the power? Surely they'd seen it, in the fight with the patrol. But no one said a thing about it. 'What happened to the Bones cats?' he asked.

'They ran away,' said Elyza Scratch. 'Like your fat friend Tam.'

So it was true: Tam had really gone. Varjak shook

his head. He couldn't believe it. What was she thinking?

'I miss her,' said Omar.

'She's a coward,' grunted Ozzie.

'We're better off without her,' said Elyza. 'We only need fighters here.'

Razor was crouched shivering behind the others. He looked naked without his ears and tail, and so much smaller than before.

'I heard what happened to Holly, Varjak,' he croaked. 'I'm sorry. I wish I could've helped her.' His voice, once so brash, was little more than a whisper. 'But Sally Bones saw straight through me. She knew I wanted to leave her gang, and join you instead.'

'Leave the Bones?' said Jess. 'Why would *you* ever do that?'

Razor touched his newest, rawest wounds. 'Varjak beat me in a fight, fair and square. He could've slashed me to pieces; he could've killed me. But he didn't.' A smile broke out on his scar-torn face. 'He's not like *her*. He's the kind of Boss I always wanted.'

Varjak looked round at his friends, embarrassed. But they were staring at Razor with open hatred.

Razor nodded at Jess. 'I'm sorry about your ear, Jessie,' he whispered. 'I didn't want them to do it.' He held out a paw to her. Jess flinched away.

'Don't touch me!' she shouted. 'It was Varjak what saved you – not me. Far as I'm concerned, you're just a big bully, and you got what you deserved!'

'But I can help you,' said Razor. 'I'd do anything to get back at Sally Bones – anything!'

'That don't make you our friend,' said Jess. 'How can we trust you, after everything you done?'

'You can't,' snapped Elyza. 'It was stupid to save him. He can't fight any more. We should leave him behind.'

Ozzie scowled. 'That's not fair.' He stood shoulder to shoulder with Razor, bristling at Elyza Scratch.

'There's no time to argue,' said Omar. 'That patrol will be back any minute, with reinforcements. Varjak: make a decision. Does Razor come with us, or not?'

Varjak tried to gather his thoughts. His face still felt raw. Up above, the red strip light buzzed on and off. He didn't know what to say. He trusted Razor; there was something in the tomcat's voice, something in his words, that rang true. But looking at Jess, with her torn ear, he knew he needed a better answer than that.

'What you said about Razor is right, Jessie,' he started. 'He was a bully, and he did terrible things, and I hated him too, back then.' Razor's fur flattened; he looked ashamed. 'But what Razor said is also right,' Varjak carried on. 'He knows Sally

Bones and her territory better than any of us. He can help us make this city free again – like your grandma wanted; like Holly wanted. I can't make you agree with me, and if you don't want him with us, then he won't come. But shouldn't we give him a chance?'

There was silence for a moment. Then, very slowly, Jess nodded. Ozzie grinned, and helped Razor up.

Elyza spat on the ground. 'You're too soft-hearted. There's no way he can help us. He's finished.' She strode towards the exit of the underpass. Malisha and Pernisha followed. Razor turned to Varjak.

'Thanks, Boss!' he croaked, his eyes wet. 'I won't let you down.'

'Good,' said Varjak. 'Because we need your help. How do we cross the river?'

'The road bridge is the best way – but it's heavily guarded.'

'That's what we thought,' said Varjak. 'So we're crossing the railway bridge.'

Razor frowned. 'No one goes on the railway bridge!'

'That's why we're doing it.'

They picked up the Scratch Sisters and left the underpass. The sun had set now. Night was drawing in. A narrow flight of steps led up to the railway bridge. Behind them, traffic screamed by in a never-ending flow.

'I haven't been here for years,' said Razor. 'We never use this bridge any more.'

'We?' said Jess suspiciously.

'I mean, they,' coughed Razor. 'You know who I mean. Trains go past all the time. If you're stuck on the bridge when one comes through – *splat*! It's over.'

'It won't be guarded, will it?' said Varjak.

'Shouldn't be, Boss. Shouldn't be. Best wait for a train to go by, and then cross right after it. We'll have to run fast. Even the biggest gaps aren't long.'

They climbed the steps. An empty, narrow platform ran alongside the railway track. They took up positions, and waited for a train. Night had fallen, and a baleful-looking moon glowered down at them. A cold wind was rising; they could hear it moaning under the bridge, chopping up the river.

Soon there was a rattling roar and an ear-splitting whistle. The platform began to shake. A train was approaching. Varjak had seen trains going over the bridge before, but from a safe distance. Now he was up close, he could feel the pressure on his face, squashing down his fur, pushing him back away from the track.

It was like a hurricane, howling through the night. The train roared towards them, its headlight blinding. The air seemed to thud and crack as it rushed by –

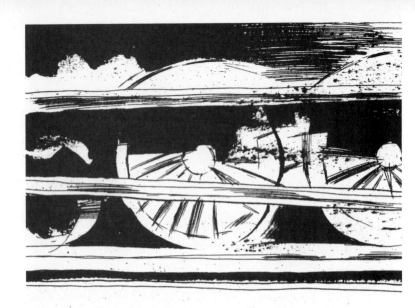

thud and crack
And Thud And Crack
AND THUD
AND CRACK

– and then it was gone, and he was looking at its red tail lights, trailing away. Varjak breathed; and only now did he realize he'd been holding his breath.

'See?' said Razor.

'It's a risk we have to take,' said Varjak.

'I don't like it,' said Elyza Scratch. 'There must another way.'

'Don't be stupid,' said Omar. 'You can see for yourself: there's the road bridge, the railway bridge, and the river.'

'Who are you calling stupid?' snarled Elyza. 'You and your brother are the stupidest cats I ever met.'

Ozzie stuck his big chest out. 'I am not stupid!'

'The way you fight!' laughed Malisha. 'No style at all! Just brute force!'

'And the way *you* fight,' snarled Omar, 'hiding behind your claws – it's for weaklings.' He looked at Pernisha, with her one ear. 'You can't even defend yourselves.'

Pernisha's pupils narrowed to slits. 'Weaklings?'

she seethed, sharpening her claws. 'Let's see who's a weakling. Let's finish this, once and for all, so everyone knows who the greatest fighters in this city are!'

'Let's!' said Ozzie, mane rippling in the wind.

Varjak's head hurt. This was impossible. If he still had the power, he could have shut them up. But he didn't. They were all bigger than him, stronger than him, tougher than him. Yet somehow, he had to get them to work together. He needed them, for without them, he'd never get near Sally Bones, and everything would be lost.

But they were cats who had never accepted any leader. They were used to living free and wild. They

didn't think they needed anything or anyone but themselves. Holly or Tam might've known how to talk to cats like this – but they were gone now, and Varjak couldn't do it on his own.

'You know what?' he said. 'If you're all such great fighters, then what's the point of me being here? You don't need me. Tam had the right idea. I'm going back.' He turned round, biting his tongue. The winter wind whipped into his ears. Below, traffic roared by, monstrous and indifferent.

'No – Varjak, wait,' called Omar.

'Come back, Paw!' said Pernisha Scratch.

He turned. They were eyeing him warily.

Razor laughed. 'Know why they're so angry, Boss? I'll tell you. It's because they know they're *not* the greatest fighters. None of them can touch Sally Bones. But you, Boss – you can, and that makes them mad. A funny-looking little cat like you – how could *you* be greater than the Scratch Sisters, or the Orrible Twins? How could—'

'That's enough, Razor!' snapped Pernisha, silencing him. She turned to Varjak, fire in her eyes. 'I'll say this much, Paw. You're the reason we're all here. You're the only one who's got a chance against the Bones. You cannot turn back from this.'

'Then do what he says,' croaked Razor, 'and stop arguing.'

'All right,' muttered the Sisters and the Twins. 'All right.'

Varjak looked at the railway track, stretching into the night ahead of him. He shivered. Razor's words weren't much comfort. He knew he wasn't the greatest fighter: not without his power, and not even with it. But Pernisha Scratch was right. There was too much at stake to turn back now.

'OK,' he said. 'Let's cross this river.'

Chapter Twenty-seven

Razor led the way onto the track, starting across the bridge at a brisk pace. It was rusty; paint was peeling off the metal. Looking down through the gaps, Varjak could see the river, moving far below.

'Quick, now,' said Razor. 'Quick.'

They raced forwards. Varjak's paw-pads stung on the cold, rusty metal; his fur ruffled in the wind. The river was so wide. Fast as they ran, crossing the bridge seemed to take for ever. Behind him, he could hear the Scratch Sisters muttering, and the Twins muttering back. The tension was still there. As long as they got over this bridge before the next train came through, Varjak didn't care. Not far now; not far . . .

'Halt!' came a voice from ahead. They were almost over the river, just a few paces from the other side. But before them now were the glinting eyes of cats. Sally Bones's cats, guarding the bridge that shouldn't have been guarded. Leading them was Uzi, one of Luger's lieutenants.

'Out of our way!' croaked Razor.

'Razor?' said Uzi. 'I don't believe it! What are you doing with those stinking outlaws?'

'Better believe it,' said Razor. 'Now stand aside!'

The Bones cats dropped into a tight defensive formation. They didn't look like they were going to back off.

Varjak frowned. He could feel the railway track vibrating, like the metal was being violently shaken. It could only be one thing: the next train coming. How were they going to get past before it came through?

'We're here to get Varjak Paw,' said Uzi. 'Sally Bones wants him, dead or alive. The rest of you can go – we'll forget we ever saw you – but Varjak Paw is ours.'

Varjak glanced around, sud-denly uncertain. What if the Scratch Sisters or Razor turned him in? But they spat at the Bones cats.

'Big words, Uzi,' said Elyza Scratch. 'Get out of our way, before you get hurt.'

'Hurt,' said Uzi, baring his teeth, 'is what we do best.'

'Please don't fight!' cried Jess. 'It's mad – can't we all just get off this bridge? I think there's a train coming—'

The vibrations were building beneath Varjak's paws, growing stronger every second. 'She's right,' he said. 'If you don't let us through, we'll all be killed.'

The Bones cats held their ground. The whole bridge was shaking now. He could hear the rattling roar, coming closer.

The train. Coming. Closer.

A headlight lit up the track in blazing colours.

Pernisha Scratch licked her lips, touched the raw end of her ear, and flicked out her claws. 'Now watch this!' she growled. 'See what a great fighter can do!'

She knifed forwards into the Bones cats, claws blurring, flashing, slashing – and ripped a hole in their defences.

Elyza burst forwards through the hole. Malisha went with her. Then Varjak and Jess, Omar and Ozzie. The Bones cats couldn't stop them. Pernisha was as much as they could deal with: the one-eared cat, on fire with vengeance.

The whole bridge was shaking and rattling, and Varjak could feel the force of the wind on his neck – but he was clear through now and running free. A platform opened up on his left. He leaped onto the platform, away from the train and its deadly wind.

He turned and saw Pernisha Scratch, proud and undefeated, still locked in battle with the Bones cats. But behind them – huge, dazzling, blinding, deafening – the train with its single headlight screamed towards them like death coming through the night.

'Pernisha!' yelled Elyza. 'Sister!'

And then the train thundered through, and Varjak couldn't see any more; couldn't hear; couldn't speak. His whole body filled with the terrible thud and crack and roar, and he could feel the wind crushing his fur as an endless chain of carriages rushed past, one by one by one, just a whisker's breadth away.

Only when he could hear once more, and the deadly wind had passed, did he dare to open his eyes. His friends were sprawled on the platform beside him. Their fur and ears were flat; their eyes clenched tight in terror.

He looked back at the railway bridge. There was no trace of the Bones cats, or Pernisha Scratch. The train had claimed them all. They were gone.

He shook his head. I can't believe this, he thought. We've crossed the river, but we've lost Tam at one end, and poor Pernisha at the other.

We're two down already – and we're not even close to Sally Bones.

Chapter Twenty-eight

'Pernisha?' said Elyza Scratch. 'Where's Pernisha?'

'She – I think the train got her,' said Malisha.

Varjak watched the two remaining Scratch Sisters search in vain for Pernisha. He could see grief rising in their eyes. The air was freezing cold. It felt like a storm was coming.

Omar and Ozzie looked at each other, tails curling round their legs. 'It's our fault,' whispered Omar. 'If we hadn't said what we said, she wouldn't have done it.'

'She went down fighting,' rasped Elyza. 'As a Scratch Sister should. But Sally Bones's gang will pay for this. We are going to make them pay – right, Malisha?'

'Right.'

Varjak could see their grief turning to fury. They flicked out their claws, and ghosted forwards. They headed towards the steps at the end of the platform.

Down on the embankment, prowling about,

Varjak could see more cats. Sally Bones's cats. He looked up. All along the riverside, those vast towers of steel and glass were glowing into the night. But like a jagged claw of darkness, that single, solitary stone tower was still far away in the distance. Sally Bones's place. Calling to him.

'Wait, Elyza,' he said. 'There are patrols down there.'

'Yes,' she replied, 'and they will pay for what happened to Pernisha.'

Varjak shook his head. 'What good will it do? If we keep fighting patrols, we'll never get near Sally Bones, and what Pernisha did won't mean a thing. Fighting won't get us there. We need something better.'

'I've got an idea,' Razor piped up.

'We're not interested,' snapped Elyza. 'Come on, Malisha. Let's go down there and wipe them out.'

'We're coming too,' said Omar. 'We will fight beside you to avenge her—'

'Wait,' said Varjak. 'We're not going anywhere till we've heard Razor's idea. Go on, Razor. Tell us.'

Razor stood a little straighter at his words. 'The Boss is right,' he croaked. 'You'll never beat them all. There's too many. But we can fool them. Sally Bones wants Varjak captured, right? She kicked me out of her gang, but I can say I want to get back in. I'll say I put together a posse with the Scratch Sisters – and

together, we've beaten Varjak, and we're taking him to Sally Bones for punishment.'

Varjak's eyes widened. It was simple, but it was good.

'I think it's really clever,' said Ozzie.

Razor's face lit up with pride. 'You leave the talking to me!' he croaked. 'They'll take us straight to the graveyard!'

'Ozzie thinks it's clever,' muttered Elyza. 'Wonderful. That's just wonderful—'

'It's this, or nothing,' said Varjak, cutting her off. 'I'm not doing it any other way.'

Elyza's eyes narrowed. Slowly, she put away her claws. 'All right, Paw. If you think it's so good, we'll try it. But the minute it goes wrong – you won't be able to hold us back.'

The air felt tight with pressure. A storm was definitely coming. Varjak could feel it in his whiskers.

'OK,' he said. 'Now, Jess, they know you're my friend, so you'll be a prisoner too. And Omar—'

Omar's tail flicked up. 'Yes, Varjak? We're in charge of the posse, right?'

'No, Omar. They know you're on my side. You and Ozzie have to be prisoners, like us.'

'Prisoners?' scowled Omar.

Elyza laughed at him. 'Get in line, scum!'

'But no one could beat the Orrible Twins!' protested Omar. 'We're the strongest!'

Lightning crackled above the city.

'Omar,' said big Ozzie, 'we're doing Razor's plan, and that's that.'

There was silence. Then thunder rumbled overhead.

'Well . . .' grumbled Omar. 'OK. But I wouldn't do this for anyone else.'

'Thanks!' said Razor, grinning. 'Now come on: everyone's got to do it right if this is going to work.' Varjak could see a bit of Razor's old confidence coming back. He still looked naked without his ears and tail – but he looked proud as he marched ahead of them all, down to the embankment.

Varjak, Jess and the Twins walked together in a huddle, pretending to look miserable and defeated. Razor swaggered ahead of them; Elyza and Malisha behind.

They were met by a patrol from Sally Bones's gang, guarding their turf with cold malevolence. It was led by Luger himself.

'Go on, Razor,' whispered Varjak. 'Make it good.'

He held his breath as the tiger-striped tomcat strutted forwards. A spike of white lightning lit the roadside.

'Razor,' snapped Luger. 'You dare show your face here?' He scowled over Razor's shoulder, and saw Varjak, and the Twins. 'What the—'

'Relax, Luger,' said Razor. 'They're my prisoners. I've captured these outlaws, and I'm taking them to the Boss for punishment.'

Luger's eyes narrowed with suspicion. The other cats in the patrol shifted about, not knowing what to think.

'I don't like this,' said Luger. 'What are those Scratch Sisters doing here? Why have you brought them onto our territory?'

'I needed them as part of my posse, to beat Varjak Paw,' said Razor. He winked at Luger. 'And

I'm taking them to the Boss, to get their just reward.'

A cold smile flickered over Luger's face. 'I see,' he said. 'Maybe you're not so bad after all . . .' Varjak felt an intense rush of relief. Razor was good; he was brilliant. They were going to get away with it. 'But something doesn't make sense here,' said Luger, scratching his head. 'What's wrong with you, Varjak Paw? Why aren't you fighting? Aren't you the cat who fights like Sally Bones?'

Varjak's heart lurched. His mind raced. And then he knew what to do: tell the truth.

'I've lost my power,' he said. 'I'm weak as a kitten now.'

'Don't get funny with me,' said Luger harshly. 'You're the cause of all this trouble. This city was peaceful before you showed up.'

'No it wasn't!' said Varjak. 'You gangs – you were—'

'Enough!' snapped Luger. 'You're nothing but an outlaw, you and that Holly you used to hang around with. Well, she got what she deserved – and so will you.'

He spat in Varjak's face. Varjak didn't respond. He had to stay calm, stay focused.

'You think you're such a hero, don't you?' Luger continued. 'You and that pathetic little Holly, break-ing the law, ruining this city for everyone else! Come on, then. If you're such a hero, hit me!' He exposed his jaw, held it out. 'Come on!'

Varjak shook his head. He was tempted, for Holly's sake. But it was better to do nothing; much, much better. Don't rise to it. Don't let it get to you.

The pressure mounted in the air. Thunder crackled in the sky.

'Scared, are you?' jeered Luger. 'You should be, because you're going to die horribly when the Boss sees you. I just wish I could kill you first, you stinking, no-good—' He slapped Varjak, flush across the face. Varjak didn't flinch, though every muscle in his body was tense.

Luger slapped him again. Varjak's face stung. Every instinct screamed at him to fight back. But we're supposed to be beaten, he told himself. I mustn't do anything, or it'll ruin the plan.

Luger licked his lips. 'Hmm. Looks like you really have lost it! So now we can do anything we like to you, and you can't fight back.'

He took careful aim – and kicked Varjak in the stomach. Hard.

Varjak doubled up in pain. He sank to the ground. Luger kicked him in the guts again. Varjak didn't move. He took the kicking. Got to stick to the plan, he thought desperately. Trust myself. That's the Seventh Skill, isn't it?

'Good,' said Luger, after one more kick. He sounded satisfied. 'Now I'm going to take you to the Boss, and she's going to punish you properly.

I'm looking forward to this.'

Omar and Ozzie helped Varjak back up. His stomach was thudding with pain; he felt like he was going to be sick; but deep inside, he was smiling. Because he knew that they'd done it. They'd fooled Luger. Razor's plan had worked.

Luger led them through the streets, towards the graveyard. This part of Sally Bones's territory was different to any part of the city Varjak had been in before. Many of the buildings here were enclosed behind high gates and fences. The windows and doors were shut, as if the people were trying to keep something out. The street lamps cast a harsh white glare. Varjak felt nervous and exposed in their light.

Luger led them on, past tall towers, through abandoned car parks sprayed with graffiti, littered with broken glass and swirling heaps of dust and debris. Finally they came to a pair of wrought-iron gates, set apart on a mound from the buildings all around.

'This is it,' whispered Omar. 'The graveyard.'

Ozzie shivered. 'I don't want to go in!'

'Wish I'd run away with Tam,' said Jess, fear flickering in her eyes.

But there was no running away from this place. They went through the gates into the graveyard. It was full of old tombstones, shrouded in snow and ice. Nothing grew here; only dead trees, their

bark turned white, their leaves long gone.

A white flash lit up the sky. It was strange to see it: the night sky, all white. No moon, no stars: just white. Against it, the criss-crossing branches of the trees looked like cracks, hairline fractures in the air.

Luger led them through the tombstones. The ground was frozen beneath Varjak's paws. It smelled dank and deadly and somehow *wrong*. His spine tingled as they stepped over the graves. Thunder cracked above their heads, like explosions in the sky.

At the end of the graveyard, the mound sloped up towards a high stone tower. It was so much bigger close up than Varjak expected. It was like a mountain: a massive, jagged claw of darkness, cutting into the night.

This was it, at last. Sally Bones's place.

At the foot of the tower prowled her gang. Dozens of cats. Their eyes glittered in the night. Varjak could smell their sharp, strong odour on the wind. At the top of the tower, there was a wide arched window with a narrow ledge. A great bell hung inside.

'So,' said a familiar voice. 'We meet again, Varjak Paw.'

Chapter Twenty-nine

It was Sally Bones. She was standing in a dark doorway at the foot of the tower, her gang ranged out
before her. She was watching Varjak with her ice-
blue eye. Her bony body gleamed white against the
doorway.

'We captured Varjak Paw, Boss,' said Luger.

'Indeed?' said Sally Bones. 'And you captured all
his gang, too?'

'No, Boss – they were guarding him. Razor put
together a posse . . .'

Luger tailed off as Sally Bones stalked towards
him.

'You fool,' she said. 'You fell right into their trap.'

The air seemed to shimmer for a moment. Then
Luger howled. There was a livid red slash on his face
– and Sally Bones was flicking his blood from her
claws.

Varjak felt Razor and the Twins flinch, but he
didn't flinch himself. He was thinking, thinking

hard, because his life depended on it. What did I do to her, last time? What is her weakness? I can't see any weakness now!

Have to get closer. That's the only way.

He took a step forwards.

'No further!' snapped Sally Bones, showing teeth that tapered down to deadly points. 'You have done well to get this far, Varjak Paw,' she said. 'You have out-fought and out-thought some of my best cats.' She smiled, though her ice-blue eye stayed cold and hard. 'So I am making you an offer. Come join my gang. Be my captain. I will give you everything you want, and more.'

She turned and nodded behind her. Some more of her gang came out of the doorway. They had a prisoner with them. A cat with spiky black-and-white fur. This cat was limping, clearly hurt – but alive. Varjak could see one of her eyes, and it was the colour of mustard. And his heart was fluttering in his chest now, like the wings of a trapped bird, because he didn't dare believe it was true.

'Holly?' he whispered.

'Yes,' said Sally Bones. 'She fell, with one of my cats. He did not survive, but his body broke her fall. She was half-conscious, calling your name, when I found her. So I brought her here, to my place. We have been waiting for you to come.'

'Holly – is it really you?'

The cat by the tower looked up. Lightning flashed above.

'Varjak?' came her voice, the gravelly voice that he loved so much, sounding as if it was coming from a huge distance, from the very bottom of the sea – but Holly's voice, unmistakably. 'Varjak, did you get away, on the rooftop? Did I do enough?'

'Holly!' he yelled, and his heart surged in his chest as he moved towards her. Up above, thunder cracked the sky. 'Yes, we made it, Holly, and it was all thanks to you!'

She smiled, spiky and beautiful as ever. But something about her was changed. He could see both her eyes now. One of them was mustard-coloured. But the other – it looked blue. Ice-blue.

'Holly, what's happened to your eyes?'

'I don't know,' she whispered. 'I've been having dreams, Varjak, such strange dreams. And now everything looks . . . different.'

'But you're alive, that's all that matters! Oh, I missed you – you don't know how much I missed you! Come on, we're getting out of here!'

'No!' snapped Sally Bones. And before Varjak could speak, half her gang stood between them again, and he couldn't even see Holly any more.

'Now make your choice, Varjak Paw,' said the thin white cat. 'You join my gang and do as I say, and you can have your friend back. Defy me, and you and every one of your friends will die.' Her tail whipped behind her. 'Choose wisely,' she said, as she turned and went back into the tower, taking Holly with her.

It was like a slash in the face.

'How dare she do that to Holly?' growled Razor. 'I say we fight!'

'He's right,' said Omar. 'It's the only way.'

But Varjak still couldn't see any weakness in Sally Bones. How could he beat her? He had to admit the truth.

'Everyone,' he said. 'There's something I've got to tell you. What I told Luger about losing the power? It's true. I've lost it.'

'Ssh,' said Jess. 'We know.'

'I've lost it, and – you what?'

'We've known for ages,' said Jess. 'It don't matter. We followed you anyway.'

'You – but – why?'

'You made us do things we never thought we'd do,' said Omar. 'Even without your power, you kept us together. You always found a way to keep us going.'

'And now,' said Ozzie, limbering his massive frame up for combat, 'we're going to do what we came here for.'

Thunder exploded up above. The Twins moved to Varjak's left. The Scratch Sisters to his right. Jess by his side. Razor behind him.

'Varjak Paw,' said Elyza Scratch, unsheathing her claws, 'the way Razor fooled Luger was genius, and I take back everything I said. But you were the one who knew. You were the one who took the kicking, to make it work. You led us here, with wisdom and courage – and you have earned the respect of the Scratch Sisters.'

'And Pernisha would say so too,' said Malisha, giving her claws one final shine.

Varjak could hardly believe it. He felt lifted by his friends, by their faith. He felt lifted; and as he breathed in, something started to happen inside him. Deep inside him, a flame leaped into life.

In–two–three–four, out–two–three–four

The world shimmered and slowed down around him –

In–two–three–four, out–two–three–four

– and he felt the power, rising in his heart again, filling his lungs, crackling from his whiskers to his tail: a hot rush that was almost more than he could control.

It was so good, this feeling. He'd missed it so much.

'Varjak!' cried Jess. 'You've got it back!'

'Yes I have,' he said. 'Thanks to you. Thanks to you all.'

He was one of a pack, and his pack was all around him. And Holly was alive! She was in the tower. He was going to get her back. This time, nothing was going to stop him.

He took a step forwards, shimmering in Slow-Time. His pack moved up with him. A snowstorm was howling down from the sky, blowing straight in their faces. Varjak didn't even notice. This was it. This was the moment.

He looked out over the graveyard. The tombstones in their crooked rows. Sally Bones's gang, ranged in their ranks. Luger stared at him, eyes full of hate.

The Bones cats unsheathed their claws. Bared their teeth. And here they came.

'GO!' yelled Varjak. His pack ran at the Bones cats – and as thunder shook the earth beneath their paws, they came together with a juddering crunch. Flanked by his friends, by a solid shield of muscle, Varjak breathed in–two–three–four, out–two–three–four, and came face to face with the enemy.

Omar and Ozzie took the first hits, on his left. They soaked them up without flinching – and struck back mightily, in an explosion of pure strength and power. The Scratch Sisters fought just as fiercely on Varjak's right – the fastest claws in town, avenging their Sister, making a way through for him.

His pack drove forwards through the snowstorm, splintering the Bones cats before them. Some tried to circle round the rear, but Razor held them off with a terrifying roar.

'Don't try it!' he yelled. 'I've got nothing left to lose!'

Varjak was fighting the fight of his life. In the middle of the battle, he led the line. He guided them into the heart of the enemy, through the grave-yard, towards the tower. All around him, his friends fought tooth and claw, every inch of the way. And inch by inch, they forced their way forwards.

'Varjak!' shouted Omar, up ahead. 'There's a gap! Go!'

Varjak looked up and saw it. Omar and Ozzie had smashed open a breach in the ranks of the Bones cats. Through that gap, he could see the dark door-way at the foot of the tower. This was his chance. This was it.

He surged forwards through the gap as Omar, Ozzie, Elyza and Malisha held off the waves of Bones cats that were closing all around them. Only Razor and Jess made it through with him.

They drove on, through the middle, through the churning mud and snow. And now another wave of Bones cats came. They were waiting; they were wait-ing; and now they came, flying through the air at him. They were led by Luger, his face a mask of blood and hate.

Razor sprang in front of Varjak. He met them head on. The tiger-striped tomcat had no ears or tail, but he would not be moved. He blocked them. He stopped them dead in their tracks. With a thunderous tackle, he smashed into Luger, and dragged him to the ground.

'Keep going, Boss!' yelled Razor. 'Keep going!'

Varjak kept going. He was clear through now, thanks to his friends; but only Jess was left beside him, and there was still another wave of Bones cats to come. He breathed deep, widened his Moving Circle out to meet them – and here they came.

One cat.

Varjak took it down.

Two cats.

Down. Down.

Three came. Three, four, five. They kept coming at him, Sally Bones's gang. Varjak got the first, got the second, spun round – and the third broke through his Circle. Claws raked his back. He kept going – so close to the doorway now, so close – but more claws were coming, ripping at his side. They just kept coming – and they were wearing him down.

Down. Varjak was down on the ground.

But little Jess – the last and smallest and weakest of his friends – tore into the Bones cats with a fury he'd never seen in her before. She startled them, just for a moment. It was enough. Varjak could move again.

He scrambled up, made another run forwards, but now there were teeth in his tail. Claws in his ribs. Paws in his face. He couldn't fight them all. His Circle broke. They just kept coming. He couldn't fight at all.

Varjak could see his friends, cut off from each other, battling for survival – not pressing forwards any more, just staying alive. He fought on, but his heart was sinking. It wasn't enough. They'd given it everything they had, they'd been magnificent, but it wasn't enough. There were just too many Bones cats. It was over, so near the end, so close. He wasn't going to make it.

'VAR! JAK! PAW!' A great roar ripped the air. A shadow soared through the snow.

'Cludge?' said Varjak. 'Cludge, is it you?'

'CLUDGE COME BACK!' barked the huge dog. 'CLUDGE COME BACK!'

And behind Cludge came another huge shadow, and another – Cludge's brothers: Buster and Bomballooloo! The three of them came roaring into the graveyard together. And at the head of them, with the biggest of grins: it was Tam!

Tam was back. She hadn't run away at all!

'Glad to see us?' she yelled. 'Thought you might need help – so I went and got some!'

The Bones cats around Varjak scattered – and now, at last, the way to the tower was clear. He dragged himself up to his paws, and made the last few steps to the doorway.

It was pitch dark in the tower. He could see the bottom of some old wooden stairs, spiralling up inside. They were very narrow; too narrow for the dogs.

Somewhere up those stairs, Sally Bones was waiting for him.

That was where Varjak had to go.

Alone.

Chapter Thirty

Varjak climbed the spiral
steps, heart thumping in
his throat.

His eyes adjusted to the darkness as he went up. The stairs were narrow, dusty and very old. There were strange carvings on the walls. They looked half-familiar, but they were crumbling, covered in cobwebs, and he couldn't see them clearly.

It was a long way up. It felt like climbing a mountain. With each step, he expected Sally Bones to come at him.

She was waiting in a chamber at the top of the tower. She was standing in front of a wide arched window, where the great bell hung. It opened onto a narrow ledge. He could see the night sky outside. He could hear the snowstorm raging; the wind howling like the end of the world. But in the tower, it was still as death and dry as dust.

Away to one side, by the bell-rope, was Holly. Sally Bones wasn't looking at her. She was staring at Varjak with her ice-blue eye. He met her gaze. It was like looking into absolute darkness, in that Mesopotamian temple chamber, before the sun came through.

He stepped forwards, shimmering in Slow-Time, the power crackling off his claws. 'It's over,' he said. 'Let Holly go.'

Sally Bones shook her head. 'You cannot beat me,' she said. 'You never could. You never will.'

'It's different now,' said Varjak. 'I know things now that I never dreamed of.'

She smiled. 'My old enemy. Come, then. Do it,

if you can.'

Varjak breathed in–two–three–four. The energy surged inside him. But the thin white cat was also in Slow-Time. Her whole body shimmered with a terrible power.

He started to circle her. There, at the top of the spiral stairs in the darkness, with the open arch behind them, they circled each other, both looking for a weakness.

Sally Bones reached out to brush Varjak's whiskers –

– and he lunged at the opening. 'That won't work any more!' he said, unleashing a Moving Circle at her. His claws lashed out, left-right, slashing, slashing. *SLASH! SLASH! SLASH!*

Sally Bones staggered back. A few strands of white fur fluttered to the ground. Their tips were red with blood.

She steadied herself and licked her lips, showing sharp pointed teeth. 'Good,' she said. 'Now do what you will. Give me everything.'

He looked into her ice-blue eye. He saw the same power that burned in him, burning like a dark star in her. It summoned something from his depths: an absolute denial. It rose up out of him, and rushed towards her.

He came at her with all his power, all his Skills, all the anger and pain and sadness in his heart. He hit her with everything: for Holly, for his friends, for the Free Cats in the harbour.

Every hit drew blood. He went for her face, her throat, her ribs, burying her in blows, ripping, smashing, slashing her apart. He'd never fought so fiercely. He had to win. So much depended on it. She had to go down.

But Sally Bones soaked it all up. She seemed to rejoice in it, as if it only made her stronger. She took everything he threw at her –

– and now she came back at him, a whirlwind of white. He parried to his left, parried to his right, but she came through the middle and kept on coming, a blur of whiteness in the dark, and he could not keep up.

SMASH!

Sally Bones broke through Varjak's Circle. His defences were breached. He reeled back, off balance.

She drove him back, and back, and back. She forced him out, through the arch, onto the narrow ledge outside the tower. Howling wind lashed his spine, froze his blood. He looked down. Through the snow, he could see the graveyard and the city lights, spread out far below. They were so high; much higher than he'd been that night when Holly fell.

Varjak's head swam. White, white snow whipped into his face. The wind was howling like the end of the world.

SLASH!

A long white claw seared through his side. He felt it, like a knife, opening him up.

He looked down, and saw a few strands of silver-blue fur fluttering away. Their ends were wet with blood.

He looked up at Sally Bones – and then she hit him: once, twice; right between the eyes.

Everything came apart. Everything broke down. Varjak spilled out onto the ledge like liquid. He felt emptied, like a black hole, a star imploding. No power left.

Can't believe it.

She's done it.

She's beaten me again.

Sally Bones stood over him, on the ledge of the tower. She was looking down at him with her ice-blue eye. She was the better fighter. She knew it, and so did he.

Sometimes, you cannot beat your enemy.

Poor Jalal. He couldn't do it. And neither can I.

Feel cold now. Everything's slipping away. It's the end of the world.

It's over.

Varjak shut his eyes, and waited.

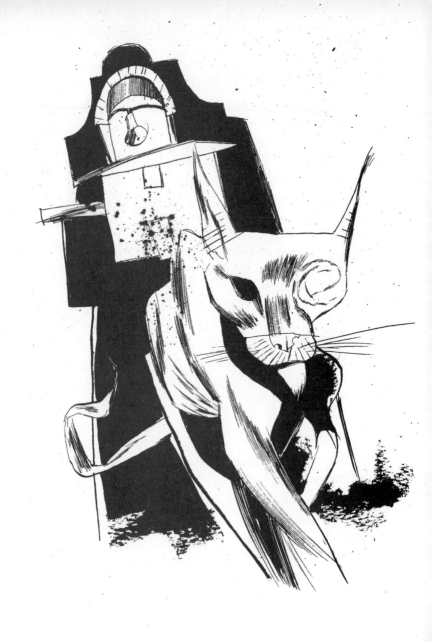

CLANG!

CLANG!

CLANG!

A vast ringing noise filled his head. At first he thought it was Sally Bones, hitting him again; but he could feel nothing – no pain, nothing. And a great tide of sound was rising, each note louder than the last, chiming, pealing, blasting into the night.

He opened his eyes. Sally Bones was standing above him. There was pain on her face; she was flinching at the noise; her ears pinned back as each clang filled the sky around them, resounding again and again, even bigger than the sky. And it hurt Varjak's ears too – it felt like it was burning into the core of his brain – but it was a glorious sound.

CLANG!

CLANG!

CLANG!

Sally Bones turned away from Varjak. Scowling with fury, she stalked back through the open arch. And in the tower –

It was Holly! She was ringing the massive bell! She was swinging on the bell rope, using all her strength to make it peal out into the night. With that glorious, deafening noise, she'd distracted Sally Bones, just long enough for Varjak to catch his breath.

'Get back in here, Varjak Paw!' yelled Holly. 'Get back off that ledge and *fight*!'

He grinned, in spite of everything.

Holly. She made something shine in him. Like fine whiskers of starlight, or a chain of coloured lights, brilliant in the winter night. Holly still believed in him, even now.

Far below in the graveyard, his friends were looking up. Every single one of them believed in him. I cannot let them down, he thought. They need me. They're my pack. My gang. I will not let them down.

But what can I do, against Sally Bones?

The only way is to face your enemy. Face them and see them truly, without fear, without hate.

Varjak heaved himself up onto his paws. His body was a wreck, a broken, bloody pulp of pain, like a train had run him over, crushed him flat into the track. His side was bleeding, his back was aching; his paws felt like they'd break if he fought any more. But he went back through the arch, and faced Sally Bones again.

The bell had stopped ringing. Its sound was still

reverberating, resonating, but it was dying away. Sally Bones had chased Holly down from the bell-rope and was shaping up to slash her to death.

'You leave Holly alone,' growled Varjak.

Sally Bones turned, and saw him, and laughed in his face. 'Varjak Paw! Back for more? What a courageous little cat you are. You fought well. I am almost sorry it must end. But end it must.'

She came up close to him; so close, he could see the bones jutting out of her; he could almost smell the darkness. But he didn't back off. He didn't breathe in–two–three–four, or make a Moving Circle. He stood his ground, still and silent, and looked into her ice-blue eye without fear, without hate.

And what he saw was Sally Bones. Everything she was, everything she used to be, everything she would be: he saw it all, and he saw it truly. This cat who'd lived so long in darkness –

– he saw the darkness –

– the despair –

'Yes,' she murmured. 'Give in to the darkness.'

But Varjak was not afraid any more. And now he remembered what he'd done, last time, in the harbour yard. He'd thought of Mesopotamia. Of the mountain. Of the bright and silent sunlight –

Sunlight.

Sally Bones was never seen in sunlight. Did it

dazzle her? Was that why she'd pulled away from him? Was she powerful only in the darkness?

One ray of light can change everything.

It was the darkest hour of the night, the hour before dawn. If he could hold on, if he could somehow hold on till sunrise, then maybe, just maybe, he'd have a chance.

So as Sally Bones came towards him, Varjak told himself what to do. Hold on till sunrise. Just hold on. Hold on and don't give up, whatever happens.

He breathed in–two–three–four, and prepared to meet her again. He stood there, shimmering with a power that came from deep within, from everything good and bright inside him.

She threw everything she had at him. All the anger and pain and sadness in her heart. All the darkness and despair in the world. Blow after blow, raining down on Varjak's head. It was all he could do to keep his Circle strong against the onslaught, to hold on, just hold on, for dawn.

He lost track of time as they fought. It could have been hours. Could've been days, or years. A hundred years, locked in battle with his enemy.

Just hold on till sunrise.

She was strong, Sally Bones. She was so very strong; and the darkness in her heart was powerful; and Varjak was tired now, so tired.

Slowly, but surely, she pushed him back, and back, and back; back onto the ledge of that fearfully high tower; and he could hear Holly ringing the bell again, but it did no good this time, because Sally Bones was pushing him back, and he knew she would not stop until he'd fallen to his death.

But still he held on. How much longer till dawn? He'd lost all sense of time and space. Where were they? It seemed like the world was flickering, blurring at the edges, its surfaces growing thin. It seemed like he could see through the world, through time and space, to something older, deeper, truer. It was almost like he could smell the sharp sweet wild mint, and see the mountain –

No. He *could* see it. There it was, before his eyes: a mountaintop at sunrise.

He was on top of the mountain, on the snow-capped ledge. And there was Sally Bones, in this secret place with him, just as he'd seen her in his vision in the pool.

The sun of Mesopotamia was rising higher in the sky. The sunlight beat down on Sally Bones, the bright and silent sunlight. It reflected off her snow-white fur. It grew brighter and brighter, more and more brilliant. And Sally Bones stepped back from Varjak, blinking in the light. She looked dazzled. She looked dazed. She closed her eye, and cried out.

'No! No! No!'

And her cry must have snapped him back to his senses, because the world grew solid again, stopped flickering, and they were back on the ledge of the tower, high above the graveyard. The city was spread out below.

But even here in the city, the sun was rising in the sky.

It was dawn. A beautiful dawn. Sally Bones was

clutching her head in the daylight. Her ice-blue eye was closed.

Varjak had made it. He'd held on till sunrise. And now he had a chance. In darkness, he knew he'd never beat her; but in daylight, maybe he was stronger than he knew.

He came at her with the last drop of strength left in him. He came at her, and she could not stop him. He drove her back, to the edge, until there was nowhere left for her to go. She looked at him one last time, with a strange expression in her ice-blue eye – and then she lost her balance, lost control, and Sally Bones, the thin white cat, she fell, and fell, and fell away from view.

He looked down from the ledge. He was so tired after the endless night, it seemed to him that the world flickered one last time, and he thought he could see her tumbling from a mountain peak, down to a sunless sea.

He never saw her hit the ground. But he saw her gang, and his friends, all staring at something in the snow. Staring and rubbing their eyes. It was hard to be certain from this height, but it looked like the body of a thin white cat, fallen from the tower and broken on the ground below.

White against white; he couldn't be sure. But buried in the white: something that might have been a chip of bluest ice, melting in the snow.

Chapter Thirty-one

It was over.

At last, it was done. Sally Bones was gone.

'Varjak! You did it! You did it!' Holly's spiky fur rippled in the sunlight as she came towards him.

He slumped down in the tower, hardly able to believe it. 'Did I really make it?' he said. 'Did I hold on till dawn?'

'You did! You beat Sally Bones!'

He shook his head in wonder. 'Couldn't have done it without you, Holly.'

'I know. Now stop bleeding! You're making a mess!'

Gently, she licked his wounds. As she did, he watched the daylight, streaming into the bell tower. He watched the dust, swirling in the light. And he watched Holly. Her eyes had definitely changed. One was mustard-coloured, the other ice-blue. It was strange; yet both her eyes were shining with new hope.

She looked up at him, met his gaze, looked deep into his eyes. It felt like she was seeing inside him with her ice-blue eye, seeing his secrets, laying him bare – just as Sally Bones had done. But this was Holly, his friend. And this time, he felt no fear, no darkness, no despair. He just felt the loveliest warmth, flowing between them once again.

She nodded. 'So you did it, Varjak Paw,' she said softly. 'You actually climbed a mountain.'

He smiled. There was so much to tell her, so much to share. 'And guess what else? We found where all the mice go in winter! It's the best hunting ever! And wait till you meet Cludge's family, and—'

'Cludge's family?'

'Yes! And I wouldn't have made it without them, either – or the Scratch Sisters – or Razor—'

'Come on,' said Holly. 'Let's go. There's not much more I can do about these wounds. There'll be scars everywhere – but you'll live.'

They limped down the stairs together, very slowly, a step at a time. It was a long way down. Varjak was so tired, and every muscle, every bone, every strand of fur ached.

But as they made it down the final steps, out of the tower, he felt lifted once again. For there were his friends, waiting for him and Holly in the grave-yard. They were going wild, cheering and whooping into the dawn. Cludge and his brothers were yelping

with joy. The Orrible Twins were dancing on the tombstones. Razor and the Scratch Sisters were dancing with them.

'I knew you'd do it!' bubbled Tam. 'I knew it, I knew it, I knew it!'

'Grandma always said he would!' purred Jess.

Sally Bones's cats were in total disarray. Her captains approached Varjak, very cautiously. They were still rubbing their eyes.

'Did he really beat the Boss?' said Luger. 'How? Nobody can beat her – she's the greatest fighter who ever lived!'

'Not any more,' said Holly. 'Varjak won. That makes him the greatest.'

'Varjak Paw!' his friends hailed him. 'Varjak Paw! Varjak Paw!'

Was he hearing right? Could he really be the greatest, after all? It wasn't possible.

But the greatest friends, the greatest pack, the greatest gang in the world? Yes. Oh, yes! No doubt about that!

A slow smile spread across his face, and he looked up at the sky. The sun was rising high. It was a beautiful morning.

'There's been enough fighting in this city,' Varjak said to Sally Bones's captains. 'There'll be no more. We're going back to the centre, and we're going in peace. The centre is our territory. You can't come and tell us what to do any more. Our law runs there now, the law of freedom. It's a free city, for Free Cats. And nothing you do can ever change that. '

Sally Bones's captains looked at each other, still dazed – and then, one by one, they stood aside. Silent, heads bowed, tails between their legs, they parted to let him and his friends go through.

Varjak and Holly led the way, with Tam and Jess beside them. Razor, the Scratch Sisters and the Orrible Twins flanked them. Cludge, Buster and Bomballooloo brought up the rear, barking happily into the dawn.

Together, they made their way out of the grave-yard, back across the river, through the streets and alleys, to the centre of their city.

Everyone was talking about how Varjak Paw beat Sally Bones. The tale would be told again and again in the times to come. It would be remembered on long winter nights. In their darkest hours, it would give them hope. For all the Free Cats, life in the city began again that morning.

As they went back to their homes, their alleys, their harbour, the sun rose higher and higher in the sky. The sky was clear and blue, and the sun shone amber in the blue. Its rays reflected on great glass towers and tall brown buildings alike. Everything gleamed in the bright, silent sunlight. The whole city sparkled and shone.

The sun began to melt the winter snow. Soon it would become a stream: a warm, clear stream of water that would wash the streets clean, then flow out through the river, to make its way in wide, strong currents, out towards the sea.

Winter was over. Spring would soon begin.

VARJAK PAW

SF Said

'There are Seven Skills in the Way of Jalal,'
whispered the Elder Paw. 'We know only three
of them. Their names are these. Slow-Time.
Moving Circles. Shadow-Walking.'

Varjak Paw is a Mesopotamian Blue kitten. He lives
high up in an old house on a hill. He's never
left home, but then his grandfather tells him about
the Way – a secret martial art for cats.

Now Varjak must use the Way to survive in a city full
of dangerous dogs, cat gangs and, strangest of all,
the mysterious Vanishings.

WINNER OF THE SMARTIES PRIZE
GOLD AWARD

'Dazzling' *New York Times*
'The cat's whiskers' *Sunday Times*

0 552 54818 9
978 0 552 54818 2

Fergus Crane

Paul Stewart & Chris Riddell

FERGUS CRANE! YOU ARE IN GREAT DANGER!
I AM SENDING HELP. Signed T. C.,
your long-lost Uncle Theo

Fergus Crane has an almost ordinary life – having lessons
taught by rather odd teachers on the school ship
Betty Jeanne, helping his mother in the bakery. But then
a mysterious flying box appears at the window of his
waterfront home – and Fergus is plunged headlong into
an exciting adventure! The box is followed by a winged
mechanical horse that whisks him off to meet his long-
lost uncle and his penguin helpers, Finn, Bill and
Jackson. Fergus finds out that his teachers are not quite
what they seem - they're actually pirates! Can Fergus and
his winged horse save his schoolmates from the far-off
Fire Island? And who else will he find there . . .?

From the creators of the bestselling
EDGE CHONICLES

0 440 86654 5
978 0 440 86654 1

DEEP FEAR

Debi Gliori

*The Strega-Borgias are back again in the
fantastically funny, chaotically exciting
and jam-packed conclusion to their
Pure Dead adventures!*

The forces of evil are converging on StregaSchloss –
demons, the Mafia, a changeling with a nasty bite –
and the wild and weird Strega-Borgias must gather
together their allies to fight back. But there are
just a few too many distractions, with Damp the
toddler-witch missing in action and a house full of
wolves and bickering teenagers getting in the way.
Can the family keep it together – even when
they're scattered over time and place?

'Irresistibly cool'
Guardian on *Pure Dead Magic*

0 385 60631 1
978 0 385 60631 8

THE
BLACK SPHINX

MATT HART

THE BLACK SPHINX is missing.
Who wants it the most?

The indomitable CALLISTO? Queen of
the Underworld SQUALIDA MACHEATH?
Or madder than a mackerel JASPER PEPPER?
Or will it be CRISPIN RATTLE,
our orphaned young hero?

But if jackal-headed gods can't stop
JASPER PEPPER, what on earth
can CRISPIN do?

Read this rip-roaring new adventure in
paperback now . . . and test your
code-breaking skills against the hieroglyphic
messages of the sphinx!

0 552 55421 9
978 0 552 55421 3

COUNT KARLSTEIN

Philip Pullman

Listen . . . Can you hear the thunder of
ghostly hooves? The Demon Huntsman
has come to claim his prey!

Who would dare to go outdoors on All Souls' Eve,
knowing that the Demon Huntsman is on the prowl?
With his pack of howling hounds, he strikes terror
into the hearts of the villagers of Karlstein. But the
evil Count Karlstein has struck a bargain with the
Huntsman – and his two young nieces are part of
that bargain! Can Lucy and Charlotte possibly
escape their dreadful fate . . .?

A dramatic tale told in words and cartoons
by Carnegie-medal winning author
Philip Pullman.

0 440 86266 3
978 0 440 86266 6